Why Not Be Honest?

Ever since that night at the lake, five years ago, she had compared every boy she met to Chase Winfield, and they paled by comparison.

And now, out of the blue, the man had returned to Silverwood Lake. He was the man in her memories, memories she hoped were buried at last. He would never know what had transpired that fateful September night, but to Diana the irony of it all was almost too much to believe.

He had been the hunter. She had been his prey. And now the hunter was back.

Dear Reader,

Although our culture is always changing, the desire to love and be loved is a constant in every woman's heart. Silhouette Romances reflect that desire, sweeping you away with books that will make you laugh and cry, poignant stories that will move you time and time again.

This summer we're featuring Romances with a playful twist. Remember those fun-loving heroines who always manage to get themselves into tricky predicaments? You'll enjoy reading about their escapades in Silhouette Romances by Brittany Young, Debbie Macomber, Annette Broadrick and Rita Rainville.

We're also publishing Romances by many of your all-time favorites such as Ginna Gray, Dixie Browning, Laurie Paige and Joan Hohl. Your overwhelming reaction to these authors has served as a touchstone for us, and we're pleased to bring you more books with Silhouette's distinctive medley of charm, wit and—above all—*romance*. I hope you enjoy this book, and the many stories to come.

Sincerely,

Rosalind Noonan
Editor
SILHOUETTE BOOKS

SRRL-7/85

VICTORIA GLENN

Mermaid

Silhouette Romance

Published by Silhouette Books New York

America's Publisher of Contemporary Romance

To my tall, handsome and charming brother
Josh

SILHOUETTE BOOKS
300 E. 42nd St., New York, N.Y. 10017

Distributed by Pocket Books

ISBN: 0-373-08386-6

First Silhouette Books printing September, 1985

10 9 8 7 6 5 4 3 2 1

America's Publisher of Contemporary Romance

Printed in the U.S.A.

Books by Victoria Glenn

Not Meant for Love (ROM #321)
Heart of Glass (ROM #362)
Mermaid (ROM #386)

VICTORIA GLENN

an award-winning writer herself, comes from a family of writers. She makes her permanent home in the Connecticut countryside, but divides her time between the East and West Coasts. She considers it essential to the creative process to visit Disneyland at least twice a year.

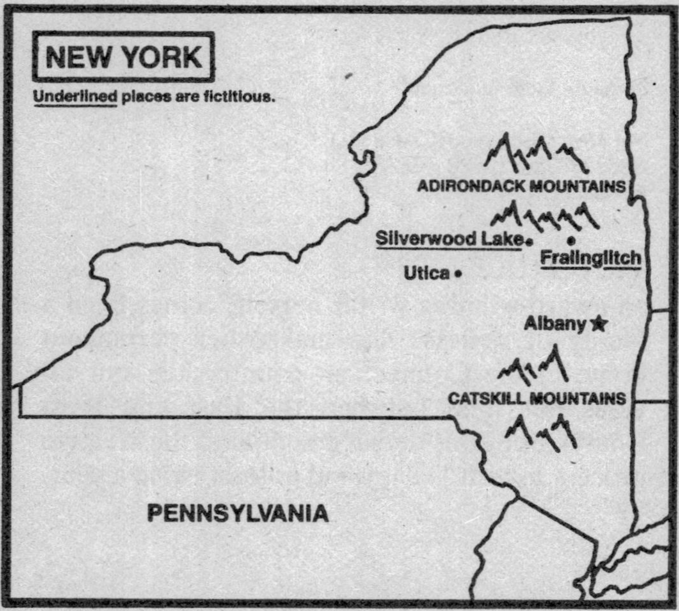
NEW YORK
Underlined places are fictitious.
ADIRONDACK MOUNTAINS
Silverwood Lake
Fralinglitch
Utica
Albany
CATSKILL MOUNTAINS
PENNSYLVANIA

Chapter One

Naturally, the news about Chase Winfield was all over the village of Silverwood Lake in a matter of hours.

"The closing was this morning," Myra MacPhee, the postmistress, was telling anyone who cared to listen. "I was right there when he signed the papers."

"I hear he paid almost twice the market value for the property," remarked Willy Sutherland, proprietor of Willy's Roadside Antiques.

Myra gave Diana a shrewd smile as she handed over the mail from her box. "Isn't that fabulous news, especially for you unmarried girls?"

"Myra, *please!*"

"Imagine having a handsome, single, millionaire right here on the lake!" Myra considered herself the town's unofficial matchmaker for the past thirty years. "I certainly do anticipate some *in*teresting goings-on!" she added with a knowing wink.

Diana groaned, and after giving Myra a feeble smile she left the postal window and walked out of the grocery store. As she emerged onto Main Street, she was greeted by the several elderly men who sat on slatted wood chairs, basking in the fading September sun. Ever since she had been a little girl, the same trio had been a part of the local landscape, growing more and more wrinkled with each passing year.

"Hi, little sweetheart!" shouted one.

She smiled. "Hello, Uncle Manny." Ever since she could remember, everyone had called him "uncle," even though he had no living relatives.

"I bet you've heard the news!" chimed in Arthur, silver-haired and extremely distinguished in his ancient plaid sport jacket.

"Oh, and what news is that?" she replied innocently.

The three men laughed. "It looks like you've got yourself a live one now! They say he's worth more than two hundred million, and that's United States *dollars,* little Di!"

She sighed wearily. When would it all end?

"But you'd better move fast if you want to beat Sara Lee Hutchins or Helga Schuyler," Uncle Manny continued. "Remember what they say about the early bird catching the worm!" The trio laughed in conspiratorial delight.

Diana laughed along half-heartedly because it was part of her upbringing never to show disrespect for her elders. Even though she was twenty-one, she was still treated like an adolescent. After all, they had known her practically since the day she was born. Besides, as far as the villagers were concerned, you weren't grownup until you were married, with at least three children.

"But we're all rooting for *you!*" declared Arthur. "I can't wait to dance at your wedding, little Di!" The others nodded, the expressions on their wizened faces almost touching in their sincere concern.

Diana finally escaped to her station wagon and turned the key in the ignition. She drove slowly past the small hub of shops, an area laughingly referred to as "the business district," pausing briefly to wave at practically everyone she passed along the way. She stopped to fill the gas tank, and realized that it was by now a foregone conclusion that Miles, the gum-chewing station attendant, would offer even more encouragement.

"I bet you're all excited about your new neighbor, hmm?" He gave her one of his gap-toothed grins. "My advice is to go straight over there tonight and borrow a cup of sugar, *if* you know what I mean!"

She rolled her eyes. "Could you check under the hood, please, and that rear left tire, I think it's a little low."

"Hmmm!" Miles raised his eyebrows in amusement. As he worked on the car Diana shook her head in resignation. How sure she had been, how very sure, that something like this would never happen. For the past fifteen years the owners of Grey Lodge had steadfastly refused to sell. Now, in a totally unexpected move, the rambling lakefront Victorian country house was now a holding of Winfield Enterprises, Incorporated. As of noon today it belonged to *that* man! Heaven only knew what he intended to do with it.

She had met him only once in her life, and it had not been a meeting in the usual sense of the word. In fact, due to the extremely bizarre circumstances, only one other person in the village was aware of what had taken place that night, five years ago. Her introduction to Mr. Chase Winfield was not what one could call proper. In fact, it had been most improper. She had been sixteen then, and it had been, to say the least, a shattering experience.

"Both of the left ones could use a little air," announced Miles, reaching for the hose.

"Fine," she murmured, returning to her thoughts. When she was sixteen the world had seemed so small and safe. Everything she knew and understood had been confined to the perimeters of Silverwood Lake. Relatively isolated from outside influences because of the absence of any large city for many miles, Silverwood Lake hosted primarily businessmen "passing through," or vacationers enroute to another destination. There was very little influx of tourism despite the awesome pine greenery because the lake was a private one. Access was limited to residents of the town only, or to those owning shorefront property. The small motel was never filled to capacity except during July and August, when parents drove to the mountains of Upstate New York from the city to visit their children at one of the two sleepaway camps, both of which had ersatz Indian names.

It was in this hottest season of the year that the clear, almost crystal lake and its surrounding woodlands were punctuated with the noisy, raucous shouts of youngsters engaged in outdoor activities. But by the last week in August the sturdy little campers all returned to their homes in the faraway cities and suburbs, and once more the lake belonged to the locals. Such was the pattern of the year and its seasons for as far back as Diana could remember. And it was on a moonlit September night, five years in the past, when she had first met an intruder in her near-perfect paradise.

After Labor Day, as was the custom, both camps were boarded up and deserted. The few vacation homes that fronted the water were also closed, with the exception of Grey Lodge. It was located at the far end of the lake, and no one had ever paid much attention to it or its residents. This was because it was usually uninhabited, except for the occasional summer or holiday rentals. Once it had been a lively place, the hub of much activity. That was when the Grey family, who had originally built the elaborate gingerbread structure, still lived there.

But nearly twenty years ago, there had been

tragedy. The only daughter of the wealthy Mr. and Mrs. Grey had gone off swimming by herself and drowned. She had been only a teenager, and her parents were virtually destroyed. They shut up the rambling home and returned to Albany, unable to bear the sight of the place ever again. Some people found it odd that the broken-hearted couple nonetheless refused to sell the property, but others found it quite understandable. Their child had been happy there, and perhaps they believed, in a strange, eerie way, she still was there. In any event, the Greys' true feelings on the matter were never revealed. But from that time on the house was made available, at a rather high rate, for those wishing to rent for brief periods of time. This usually meant rich sportsmen who chose to vacation there at whim, or the rare weekend party. It was at such a party that Chase Winfield happened to blunder into Silverwood Lake.

Diana's mother, widowed several years before, had been forced to spend a week caring for an ailing older sister in Monticello. She had left her daughter alone at their own rather comfortable house on the lake after exacting a somewhat long list of promises from Diana. No, she would absolutely *not* have any boys over to the house. No, she would absolutely *not* wear those atrocious blue jeans to school, and no, she would absolutely *not,* under any circumstances, even consider swimming alone, especially at night. Well, rules were meant to be broken, she decided about two evenings later as she dug her toes into the cold, damp sand and continued to peel off the layers of clothing.

She had been brought up so strictly, so protected, that it was the natural reaction of a teenager suddenly left on her own. This first taste of freedom was just too tempting for Diana. She had always resented being known by her schoolmates as a Miss Goody Two-Shoes. Here at last was a chance to do something simply because it had been forbidden. Knowing her little act of defiance would never be discovered made the prospect of a midnight swim exceedingly attractive. Not only would she swim alone at night, but she would do it without a bathing suit. It would be *her* little secret. She had slipped off the rest of her clothes, hesitating only for a moment before at last stripping away the cotton panties and plain white bra. At sixteen her body was already very well-developed. She left the two huge silver-toned combs in her long brown hair, and walked quite unselfconsciously to the water's edge. She shivered at the initial cold sting as the waves began to lap around her feet. Actually, the water temperature was the highest it had been that summer, and in another moment her body had already adjusted. She waded farther along the pebbly bottom until she stood knee-deep in the water. Placing her hands on her hips, she gave a sigh of satisfaction. Tonight this was her own private world, her personal swimming pool.

At this late hour all the regular residents of the

lake were long asleep. The only sounds she could hear, besides the crickets and owls, were coming from Grey Lodge, off in the distance lengthened by the veil of night. She could barely make out the lights on in the faraway windows, although one of them must have just been opened, because at once she could hear the trickle of men's laughter and the sound of a piano. Vaguely, she remembered hearing in the village that the lodge was being used by some well-heeled young businessmen for a bachelor party. Now the music became louder, and so did the laughter. She twisted her lips in amusement. They were probably showing dirty movies, or drinking to excess, or whatever rich, sophisticated gentlemen did at stag parties. Who cared, anyhow? They were much too far away to even see her, and they were all indoors besides. She tried to shut the noise out of her mind. As she walked even deeper into the water, she felt the bottom change to a mushy, muddy consistency. Turning over on her back, she kicked away toward the center of the lake, gliding peacefully along with clean strokes of her arms. It was delicious, floating serenely in the water, enclosed by the soft cocoon of night. With her head tipped back she could stare up at the full moon, an orb so bright and lustrous, it served to make the mood even more intimate and mystical.

She ducked down into the water and splashed vigorously, laughing half-aloud at the pleasure of it all. Because of the splashing she didn't hear the approaching boat, nor was she aware of the astonished expression on the face of the man who held the oars—not until it was too late, and he was merely yards away from her.

"Well, what do we have here, a mermaid?" said a deep, silky voice. Startled, she looked up and that was when she saw him. A man of about thirty, dressed in a dark tuxedo, the top several buttons on his ruffled white shirt undone, and the black tie hanging loose. There was a harshness to his near-handsome face. The slurring of his speech obviously indicated that he had had a great deal to drink. He was far from sober, she thought, and he was narrowing his eyes to peer at her in fascination. "It *is* a mermaid!" he exclaimed, following her with the boat until he was practically on top of her.

She was panic-stricken. Hopefully, in the dim light he couldn't see that she was completely nude. Unfortunately, the moon might have been a lamppost. She slid quickly down until the water covered her up to the chin.

"A mermaid without any clothes!" he declared, in a tone that was beginning to frighten her. She continued to swim away, but he was gaining on her. "Where are you going, little fish? Come back here or I'm gonna have to catch you!"

Oh, great, she thought. All she needed was to be chased by a drunk in a rowboat who was far-gone enough to believe he was actually seeing a mermaid!

"Come back here, mermaid!" the man called out.

He was close enough to practically touch her, and she was terrified. "I've got you now!" he cried, leaning over in the boat to swoop her up in his arms. She gave a last, desperate kick of her feet, and pushed just far away enough to elude his grasp.

He laughed. "You slippery little creature! I'm still gonna get you!" He stood up unsteadily in the small boat, completely unconcerned by the fact that it started to rock crazily back and forth. "I saw a mermaid swimming there, I grabbed her an' she wasn't there!" he recited with a low laugh. He bent over precariously and stretched both arms out again. "Pretty little mermaid, with little bright mermaid combs in your dark mermaid hair!"

Oh, God! Why hadn't she listened to her mother? Wasn't she always right, darn her! What had possibly possessed her to be so incredibly stupid, so reckless, going skinny-dipping alone like this? There were sharks in the water tonight. Six-foot-tall, woman-eating sharks dressed in tuxedos! And she was such a terrible swimmer. She'd never be able to elude him!

"Jus' a little closer and I've got you!" came the triumphant male voice. Its very confidence frightened her in a way she'd never been frightened before. It reminded her of the tone she had heard in hunters' voices just after they had taken aim at a duck or a moose and were about to open fire. For the first time in her young life she felt like a wild animal, stalked prey that had just been cornered. Frantically, she knifed her legs through the water, making one final effort to escape him. She did not see the intoxicated man teetering along the edge of the lightweight aluminum boat, nor did she hear his sharp, guttural cry as the small craft pitched sideways and flipped completely over, hurling him into the lake with one swift motion. What she *did* hear was a rather loud splash and the sputtering cough of a man spitting out mouthfuls of water.

Good, she remembered thinking as she turned back to see the drenched maniac struggling to keep afloat, flailing both arms about in the water. *Good, I hope he drowns,* she thought with a smirk, continuing to widen her distance from him.

"Mermaid," the voice filtered toward her, "I forgot to tell you that I can't swim!"

He was lying! He had to be! It was a trick, she decided quickly, and she certainly wasn't going to fall for it. But a split second later she paused instinctively, her ears alert.

"Uh, I guess the truth is . . . never took the time to learn!" There was a black humor to his voice, and he began to choke in spasms. "Some . . . joke, mermaid!" he coughed. "I guess the"—he gasped—"the last laugh is on me, huh?" That was when she saw him go under for the first time and realized that the crazy fool really *couldn't* swim!

Diana sprang into action and frantically swam back toward the drowning man. She reached him just as he was going down for what might very well have been the last time and grabbed hold of him by the slippery lapels of his now-ruined jacket. He was a large man, and in his water-logged evening clothes it was a struggle just to keep him afloat. Protectively, she held his head above the water with one arm as she paddled toward the shoreline with the other. His body was practically limp, almost a dead weight. He seemed to be barely conscious of what was happening. Diana was swallowing mouthfuls of water herself as she fought her way to the shallow with her unexpected burden. It seemed like hours, but in reality only minutes had passed before her feet rested, at last, on the muddy bottom. Breathing heavily, she wrapped her arms around his torso and pulled him onto the sandy beach. He fell back, and water trickled out of his mouth. His eyes were tightly shut. Quickly, she flipped the man over on his stomach and began to push the water out of his lungs. He gave a weak cough, and then began to heave.

Seconds later, with relief, she could hear him sucking up huge gasps of air. He was breathing, thank God! Rolling himself over onto his back, the man's eyes began to open and focus a little hazily on the sight of the girl leaning worriedly over him. "Mermaid?" he whispered in disbelief.

"You . . . you'll be all right now," Diana assured him gently, pushing back the soaking black hair from his face. His eyes, she noticed for the first time, were a strange hue of silver, or maybe it was the reflection of the moon. He had a hard, gaunt face, but the eyes stared up at her with incredible tenderness. "Mermaid, you're so beautiful!" he murmured softly. He closed his eyes with a deep sigh as Diana continued to stroke his wet hair. "And your touch is so sweet."

She froze, suddenly shocked back to reality. Her attempts to soothe him had merely been instinctive on her part. She was reacting to the immediate danger that had just passed and she touched him the way she might have comforted a crying child or lost animal. But now she realized that this was a full-grown man, and it was midnight on a deserted beach, and she was completely naked! Quickly, she stood up, and retreated several feet back into the shadows.

"Where—where are you going?" the man called out dizzily. With a strength Diana didn't think he possessed, he propped himself upright and moved along the cool sand toward her. She crouched behind a small boulder in an attempt to hide herself. The rock concealed her body from the hips down.

"Beautiful mermaid . . ." he repeated, shaking his head, "please don't . . . don't swim away again!" He ran his silvery eyes, with that strange glint in them, over her. His lips broke into a smile, and with one hand he reached out at her. "Now that I've found you I won't let you go away!" But just at that moment, when he might have touched her, his hand fell limply to his side and his eyes rolled shut. With a sigh his head lolled back, and then his body tumbled over into an unconscious heap. Soon came the sound of soft, steady snoring. He had passed out cold, she realized with relief. Well, what was she going to do now? She couldn't just let him lie there all night in those wet clothes. He could get pneumonia!

Rapidly, she made her decision. First, stumbling back to her own property, she found her abandoned pile of clothes. Quickly, she pulled on her jeans, sweatshirt, and old torn sneakers. Her socks, panties, and bra she merely rolled into several tight balls and stuffed them into her pockets impatiently. In a situation like this, particularly after midnight, there was only one person she could depend on. Three houses down lived old Pete Turner. As she ran along the woods into his yard, Pete's myopic dog, which was practically as old as its master, began to bark excitedly.

"Would you shut up, Hans," she whispered urgently. "You want to wake up the whole world?" She darted up the back porch and began tapping lightly on the screen door.

"Pete, are you up?" Lights were switched on inside the cottage, and Hans continued to bark with delight at the unexpected company. He jumped eagerly up and down around Diana's legs in playful abandon. "No, I can't play with you now, you dumb animal!" she groaned.

Just then the door flew open and a sleepy-eyed Pete gazed out at her. "Diana?" He scratched his head. "Are you all right, honey?"

She nodded, and as quickly as she could managed to tell him all about the man who lay unconscious on the beach. At once alert, Pete disappeared into the house and in a matter of moments emerged fully dressed, arranging his faded red plaid shirt over his huge stomach, and tucking it into his rumpled khaki pants. Grabbing the flashlight that hung suspended over the hook by the door, he followed her back through the woods. When they arrived at the spot where the huddled form lay sleeping, Pete gave a low whistle and scratched his head again. Hitching his flashlight into a loop of his baggy slacks, he bent over and gripped the man under his arms.

"You take his legs, honey," he ordered, and slowly they made their way back through the soft sand, around the tangling branches, and finally back up the steps into his house.

It wasn't long before Pete had stripped off all the man's soaking clothes and wrapped him in several warm blankets as he continued to sleep peacefully on the threadbare chintz sofa in the small living room.

"I can pretty much guess what happened," he remarked dryly to Diana as they both stood drinking coffee in the kitchen. "He was at that party, pie-eyed, and decided to take a little boat ride. You were out there takin' a little swim." He smiled. "And after what your mama told you—"

"You aren't going to tell her, are you?" she pleaded.

He shook his head. "It was a stupid thing to do . . ."

"You *are* going to tell her—"

". . . but you learned your lesson." He smiled.

"Nah, why would I tell on you?" There was a pause. "Only thing is, *this* one better not ask any questions. Do you have any idea who he is?"

"Should I?" Diana was puzzled.

"Well"—her friend hesitated—"I saw him when he came into the village with some of his pals this afternoon. His pictures been in all the papers, and besides, I heard them say his name once or twice. He's Chase Winfield."

Chase Winfield! His name was well-known by the local residents, who voraciously read the glossy personality magazines on the stands at Myra MacPhee's grocery store. Chase Winfield, self-made millionaire, a wunderkind with the microchip. The tiny company he'd started on a shoestring barely ten years earlier in California's "silicon valley" was now one of the most highly innovative voices in the entire computer industry, and Winfield Enterprises, Inc., had expanded into other unrelated ventures, even more successful. The man, it was rumored, had a Midas touch. But what made him especially interesting to the female population of Silverwood Lake were his widely publicized liaisons with an assortment of famous cover girls and lovely young film and television actresses. A true-blue American playboy, this Chase Winfield.

Diana felt a heaviness in her stomach. What if the newspapers got hold of what had happened? It could occur easily enough, and she couldn't bear thinkingabout the publicity. *Unclad Teen Saves*

Drowning Playboy! Just wonderful. She'd never live it down. Never mind about her mother, who would probably ground her for the next three years.

"Don't worry," assured Pete, as if he could read her mind. "This Winfield guy is down for the count. I doubt he'll remember anything that happened in the past couple of hours. But if he does"—there was a pause—"I'll tell him he was seeing pink elephants or something."

"Pete," she confessed hesitantly. "You see, the thing is, I wasn't wearing, I mean—"

He waved his hand. "I know, honey. You don't have to tell me."

"But you don't understand—" she protested.

"Sure I do. Who wears a bathing suit for a secluded midnight swim?" He grinned. "Besides, what's that stuff dangling out of your pockets?"

Mortified, Diana shoved the protruding undergarments back into her jeans pockets. "Uh, listen, Pete, I really appreciate—"

"Forget it, honey. Now, shoo! Get outta here!" He good-naturedly pushed her out the door.

"Thanks again," she called from the steps.

"For what?" Pete pointed a finger. "Nothing happened, do you understand? You didn't go swimming tonight. You didn't see a guy fall out of a boat. You didn't pull him back to shore. Get it?"

"But—"

"No buts! That's what happened, nothing! I happened to be taking Hans for a stroll by the lake and I saw this guy washing up on the shore, drunker than a skunk. I carried him back to the house and here he is now. End of tale." The heavyset older man smiled. "It was all a dream. Go back to bed." He disappeared back inside and closed the door.

Diana trudged home and crawled into bed. When she woke up the next morning it all did seem rather like a dream. A rather crazy dream. She didn't set foot outside until it was time for school Monday morning. By then, the entire bachelor group had packed up and returned to the city. Pete later told her that Chase Winfield had seemed a bit bewildered when he awakened. But fortunately, he accepted Pete's version of the events of the previous night. In gratitude he even offered Pete a rather substantial renumeration for his kind deed. The older man, of course, was not interested. Money meant absolutely nothing to him. It never had.

As far as Diana was concerned, there was virtually no likelihood of Chase Winfield ever crossing her path again. After all, he had only been a member of a wedding party, the best man, in fact, she later learned from a photograph in a major news magazine. The incident gradually faded into what would merely remain a bizarre, disturbing memory.

"I said, that's ten seventy-five for the gas, Diana!" repeated Miles, snapping his gum with good-natured impatience.

"Oh, sorry," Diana said, jarred back to the present. She handed the freckle-faced young service station attendant some bills and waited for her change.

"Here you go, Diana," said Miles, returning from the cash box and counting out the money. He winked as she drove off. "Don't forget my advice about the cup of sugar!" he yelled after her.

Chapter Two

Diana turned the car off the Old Lake Road and into her own driveway. It was a narrow dirt track that twisted and curved for over a quarter mile, threading its way around tall pines and gnarled old elms. She had never failed to marvel at the awesome natural beauty when approaching her lakeside home. Of course, during the winter she never failed to marvel at the awesome inconvenience of being stranded until Miles and his snowplow arrived and cleared away the ten-foot drifts in her driveway.

Pulling up to the small two-story white house with its fading green shutters, she turned off the ignition, and gathered up her groceries. Critically, she surveyed the peeling railing on the front porch. A paint job was crucial before the cold weather set in. She'd simply have to stop procrastinating and borrow that ladder from Pete. When her mother had suddenly passed away two years ago, Diana was a junior at one of the state colleges, still working on her nursing degree. It had been extremely difficult to keep up the house in the same meticulous fashion as her mother had, especially living in a dormitory more than a hundred miles away. Now she unlocked the door, which needed oiling, and set her packages down on the kitchen table, which desperately needed refinishing. She sighed.

The kitchen floor needed waxing, the old gas oven needed cleaning, and it had been a year since anyone had touched the top of the refrigerator. Never mind about the three days worth of dishes in the sink.

"Sorry, Mom," she addressed a snapshot clipped on the freezer door with a fruit-shaped magnet. Fondly, she brushed the thin film of dust off the color photo of her and her mother taken four years ago at her high school graduation. Diana was in her white robe and mortarboard with her arm around her proud mom, dressed in her best blue silk, with a white corsage pinned at the neckline, a traditional gift from all graduating seniors to their mothers. What a happy day that had been. She shook her head in fond memory, still seeing Myra MacPhee reaching for Diana's camera and hearing that clarion voice of hers booming in every direction.

"Linette, brush the hair out of your eyes! Diana, put your arm around her and try to smile, would you?"

Try to smile. That was something that had never

come easy to Diana. In the past few years she'd really made an effort, especially while away at school. These days, though, there didn't seem to be very much to smile about. She was more lonely than she'd ever been. Half of her classmates from high school had married within a year after graduation and were well on their way to starting families of their own. Many others had simply moved away from Silverwood Lake in search of greener pastures, better opportunities. And who could blame them? There wasn't very much to do here, unless a person wanted to work on the family dairy farms or in one of the many apple orchards that ringed the area. Of course, there were several small factories in the vicinity, but they were light industry and not employers on a grand scale. Besides—she twisted her lip—how many men had an aching desire to work in a doll factory?

She had been home since commencement in May, and immediately began working in the county health clinic. This was a career that had been planned for her when she had been barely five years old. She had been an excellent student, and so it surprised no one when she received a partial scholarship to continue her studies at the university. She had always wanted to become a nurse, and she'd never contemplated working outside Silverwood. Dr. Myers had delivered her twenty-one years before. His old nurse had retired, and Diana slipped right into the routine as if she'd been there for years. Strangely, something about it all made her feel older than she was. Sure, she enjoyed the work, and Dr. Myers was a gentle old soul, but after three months she was starting to feel an odd restlessness.

This afternoon, when after five years she'd heard the name of Chase Winfield spoken aloud, the restlessness had suddenly been replaced with a knot in the pit of her stomach. Would she run into him ever? Of course, how could it be avoided? Would he even remember her? Very unlikely, after all these years, and besides, the entire episode was probably one great blur to the man. Still, it was embarrassing to envision meeting Chase Winfield. He represented the polished, sophisticated man of the world and everything about him intimidated Diana. Who was she, after all? Diana Mueller, who even after four years in a bustling college town *still* remained a virgin. Diana Mueller, who despite being considered somewhat pretty, had gone on a total of seven dates since high school, five of them during her freshman year of college.

She climbed upstairs to the bedroom that had been hers since childhood. The narrow bed still had its pink canopy and matching flounce. Every doll and book she'd ever been given stood on the rows of the built-in shelves. How she'd always loved the way the ceiling of the room sloped down at the sides, and the perfect way the faded flowered wallpaper followed the motion. Her father had lovingly cut and pasted the paper when Diana was barely six years old. He'd even let her help him press the sides down with a roller. After all this time the edges were starting to peel off slightly, but she would never repaper this room. Not in a million years. There was far too much affection captured in those tiny little pink rosebuds, even as they slowly paled, year after year, against the yellowing background.

Diana kicked off her white shoes, and then peeled off her immaculate pants and matching smock. She walked over to the mirror on the bedroom door and examined her features dispassionately. Of medium height; hair, medium length; eyes, medium color; figure average. Everything about her—average. Nothing truly exceptional at all. Oh, well. Maybe there was something reassuring about being unexceptional. Not everybody could look like Helga Schuyler! She smiled, recalling the spectacular, blond, willowy Helga, a year ahead of her in high school. It was one of the village's all-consuming mysteries why the statuesque beauty was still unmarried. It was hardly a mystery to Diana. The truth was, there wasn't much of a selection left for unmarried girls in their early twenties. If a young man wasn't settled soon after high school, it wasn't likely that he was worth settling with. The attrition rate was appalling, with so many young people moving away to the city in search of livelier times and better opportunities. Helga Schuyler could have her pick of what remained, but failed to find anything worth picking.

Well, Diana thought cynically, Helga's prospects had certainly brightened since this morning. Like every other man in town, Chase Winfield would quite likely be bowled over by Helga's aloof beauty, but who could tell? After all, Helga might be a knockout by Silverwood Lake standards, but up against the glamorous and alluring women in Mr. Winfield's worldly orbit, she was just another gorgeous face.

In any case, what was it to her what Chase Winfield did or did not do? Just so long as he didn't start having outrageous orgies at Grey Lodge. How intolerable it would be if anything should happen to alter the easy, peaceful, simple lifestyle on the lake. Silverwood was a sleepy little village, and she had come to take tranquility for granted. Loud, unruly disturbances coming from the direction of Grey Lodge would most certainly not be welcome. Diana's mouth tightened. Just let that outsider come in here and try to ruin the place. She paused. How could she ever expect to go one-on-one against a man as powerful as Chase Winfield? Had she forgotten so quickly how overwhelming he had seemed to her five years back? True, she had been just a frightened teenager, and he was a dark, intimidating stranger, but the fact remained that the man had conveyed an unmistakable dynamism even then. They said he was a barracuda in the business world. He could probably eat her for breakfast. Just imagine how intimidating he would be sober. The very thought of another run-in with him made her cringe involuntarily. She went over to the closet and pulled an old T-shirt and pair of jeans off their hangers. She then slid on her favorite grubby sneakers. She'd better get that ladder from Pete's garage before dark.

As Diana weaved her way through the thick underbrush by the lake's edge toward her neighbor's cottage, she couldn't help peering off in the distance at the rambling old Victorian lodge. Already the new owner's occupancy was evident by the presence of a sparkling white motorboat. No doubt, the high and mighty Mr. Winfield intended to gift the water with with his very own expensive oil slick. Rich people! They never considered the possibility that their own rather extravagant and careless lifestyles might be in conflict with the so-called "lesser" people.

Hans was barking his usual wild greeting. He was practically blind these days, but Diana's scent was far too familiar ever to be forgotten. He jumped, although not as high as he used to, and joyfully pushed his paws against Diana's shins. Affectionately, she ruffled his shaggy fur.

"Is your daddy home, hmm?" Diana scoured the area around the small cottage. Pete's old pickup was nowhere to be seen. Diana sighed. He was probably still in Fralinglitch, getting more fishing supplies. Of course, she was welcome to her friend's home anytime, to help herself to anything she desired, but still, it would have been easier if Pete had been there to help her carry the bulky ladder. She pulled open the huge gray door to the detached garage and fumbled in the musty space until she at last spied the folded aluminum ladder. Dragging it clumsily through the underbrush back toward her own property, she lost her footing and slipped.

"Ouch!" she exclaimed angrily, dusting her jeans off and vainly attempting to shake the pebbles out of her sneakers. This was going to be more difficult than she had anticipated. She took a breath and reached for the ladder again. This time she must have gone about twenty yards before a branch snapped back and hit her squarely in the face.

"For crying out loud!" she declared, her cheek stinging. Helga Schuyler wouldn't have these problems. Of course, Helga never had to paint her own house, did she? Helga had big, strong brothers to carry ladders for her. Hans, who had followed her this far, couldn't quite understand what the difficulty was. All he could see was that Diana had stopped whatever it was she had been doing, and so, therefore, it must be time to play. He approached her hopefully, with a small stick in his mouth.

"If you really want to play fetch, how about just fetching me somebody to help carry this stupid ladder?" she murmured irritably.

"In need of assistance?" a deep voice suddenly asked.

Diana stared up in astonishment at the man standing barely yards away. He was tall and lean, casually dressed in jeans and a sweatshirt. Something about his tanned, hard face was disturbingly familiar.

He came closer, his silvery glance flickering over her briefly, then pausing for just a moment at her face. "You've cut your cheek," he said, reaching into his pocket and pulling out a handkerchief.

"I'm okay," she replied quickly, averting her gaze and quickly bending down over the aluminum ladder. That voice! Of course, who else could it be? Chase Winfield!

All at once a firm, strong hand stilled her arm and the weight of the burden shifted from her. She looked up through her curtain of hair to see Chase Winfield hoist the ladder to one side. "You don't look okay to me," he observed quietly, pushing aside the silky strands of brown hair to dab gently at the long red scratch.

She winced involuntarily. "Thank you." The touch was so unexpectedly soothing.

"I couldn't help overhearing," he was saying in that well-remembered tone of his. "You seemed to be having a little difficulty."

"Not at all, I'm just fine," she replied so hastily that the man quirked an eyebrow in curiosity. He stopped his ministrations on her injured skin and handed her the soft cotton square.

"Let's not be ridiculous," he countered brusquely, lifting the ladder up onto his shoulder in one easy motion. "Lead the way."

She shrugged in protest. "This isn't necessary."

"Since I just happen to be taking a walk around the lake, it's no trouble at all." He paused. "I assume you have a name?"

"Diana," she said as she swallowed the lump in her throat.

"Well, Diana, I'm Chase. I guess we're neighbors."

There was no way he could possibly have recognized her, even if, by some freak chance, he remembered what had occurred all those years ago. Strangely enough, it was through this very underbrush that she and Pete had dragged the unconscious man. Coincidence, of course.

"So here I am, trying to be neighborly, Diana. How about steering me and this ladder in the right direction?" There was just the slightest trace of impatience in his voice.

"This way," she pointed quickly, leading him through the woods toward her own house. He followed her across the lawn to the back porch, and paused questioningly.

"Anywhere over there would be just fine," she said.

He propped the ladder up against the side of the structure and brushed his hands off on the blue jeans, which Diana now noticed were the expensive, well-fitting designer kind. His sneakers, too, were brand new, and obviously expensive, with that distinctive leather trim. He wore it all with the special air of a man who took it for granted that he always looked his best.

"Thank you very much, Mr. Winfield," she said, almost without thinking.

The side of his mouth twitched. "So you know my

last name?" There was an amused pause. "I don't know why I should be surprised. This is a very small town." He pushed his hands into his hip pockets. "There's probably not much else to talk about around here."

"Mr. Winfield," she replied sweetly, "believe me, there is *nothing* else to talk about." Her frankness seemed to astonish him for a moment. He looked around at the house and at the tall pines next to it.

"Diana, I don't suppose your family would be interested in selling."

She was taken completely off guard. "Selling what?"

"Your property." He eyed the porch critically. "To be frank it's a bit rundown."

"*Rundown?*"

". . . But rest assured, I'd give you a fair price for it."

The nerve of that man! She'd been right all along about him. A real barracuda. Diana was so taken aback, she completely forgot about her natural shyness. "Who do you think you are that you can just come in here and buy up everything?" Her eyes blazed. "You're unbelievable, you know that? Absolutely unbelievable!"

There was a long, uncomfortable silence, and the muscles on his face tightened. "Forget I asked," he finally retorted harshly. "I didn't come here to have my head bitten off."

"What *did* you come here for?" Heavens, what

was wrong with her? She'd never been so rude in her entire life.

"Look, young lady, I was just helping you with that ridiculous ladder—"

"I mean, why did you come *here*, to Silverwood Lake?"

He glared back at her. "I don't believe that's any of your business, now, is it?" He turned swiftly and stalked away, disappearing into the underbrush.

Diana shook her head angrily. Just who did Chase Winfield think he was? But actually, she was more angry at her own ill-mannered behavior. Very nice, she told herself. *Yes, you certainly know how to win friends and influence people, Diana! No wonder you have such a busy, active social life.*

She retreated back into the house and flopped down on the corduroy living room sofa. The truth was that Chase Winfield had first disarmed her with his seemingly gentle concern, and then . . . She looked down at the folded, neat linen square still in her hand. The superbly embroidered initials CPW stared up at her from one of the white corners. The man had spoken with apparent sincerity about being "neighborly," and then he turned around and without so much as a thought tried to acquire her property. This sudden development was quite distressing. Why would he want her land also? If he had purchased Grey Lodge simply as a vacation retreat, surely he already owned adequate lake frontage for his needs. But what if he had a totally different purpose in mind? In Diana's worst dreams she had always feared developers coming in and taking over the lake, changing its tranquil face forever.

What was his plan? She had to find out somehow. She had to know what Silverwood Lake was up against.

"Damn you, Chase Winfield," she whispered, punching one of the cushions. "I never should have pulled you ashore that night! If I'd just let you sink to the bottom of Silverwood Lake, we wouldn't be in this predicament now. It's my own fault!"

Chapter Three

Dr. Myers was semi-retired and did not have Saturday office hours, so Diana had the entire weekend off. When she awoke in the morning, the September sun was flooding brightly through the bedroom window.

"I don't want to paint today!" she murmured into the muslin pillowcase. Well, Myra MacPhee certainly had one point about marriage. At least a person who was married had someone else to talk to. She didn't have to go around talking just to dogs, refrigerator doors, and pillows. This was starting to get a bit ridiculous. Diana finally stretched and hauled her protesting body out of bed. No, today she would have to start the paint job on the exterior. Perhaps she was getting maudlin, but more and more, whenever she did household tasks that were normally considered the man's prerogative, she would start wondering what it would be like having a husband to do them. Diana hated being wistful about such matters. After all, there hadn't been a man around this house since Dad had died ten years earlier. To be honest, though, she had felt a bit cheated, with just herself and Mom struggling with the heavier chores. Good old Pete Turner, though. He always seemed to be there without being asked, taking care of a leaky faucet or a loose shingle. But this time her pride would not permit imposing any more tasks on her good-natured friend. She'd do it herself and get it over with, period.

After grabbing a doughnut and some cold milk, which immediately formed a hard ball that sank to the bottom of her stomach, Diana threw on her oldest, dingiest T-shirt and hitched up the shoulder straps on her faded denim overalls. She paused in front of the bedroom mirror and secured her glossy hair with two pink plastic ponytail clips. Critically surveying her appearance, she flung her hands up in the air.

"Elegant as always, Diana!" she declared to her reflection. At least she had beautiful skin, and her lashes were dark enough so that she could usually get away without mascara. In college the joke among her friends had always been, "What does Diana call 'formal?' "

"A T-shirt that isn't inside out." Very droll. But it

was the truth. Except for when she was on duty at the clinic, her mode of dress was decidedly casual. And around here, what was there to get dressed up for? She paused. Better make that *whom* was there to get dressed up for?

She grabbed her oversize sunglasses and walked out to the car. How magnificent the lake looked this morning! Fall had definitely come early this year. Already the elms and maples were tinged with orange and yellow, casting their confettilike reflections on the glimmering waters. The pines, however, stood their ground—green, tall, and cool. The entire autumn scene washed together like a French Impressionist painting. *Please,* she silently prayed, *don't let anything or anyone ever destroy this exquisite natural beauty!*

Again her thoughts returned to Grey Lodge and its new resident. How could she manage to find out what had really motivated Chase Winfield to purchase the old Victorian house? He was a multimillionaire; he could live anywhere in the world he wished. And frankly, even though she personally considered the house lovely and the scenery magnificent, her own opinion was heavily influenced by sentiment. There were an infinite number of settings just as beautiful throughout New York State, and houses far more attractive than Grey Lodge. It simply didn't make any sense that a man like Chase Winfield would choose as his vacation home a charming but unspectacular place in the middle of nowhere. It wasn't as if he had any special ties to the village. As far as she knew, he'd been here only once before, during that fateful weekend five years ago. Obviously, he hadn't purchased the property for sentimental reasons, since Chase Winfield was hardly known as a sentimental man.

Diana slid into the driver's seat and slammed the door with annoyance. Those final words they had exchanged had been so harsh, so bitter. He was certainly a man who liked getting his own way. Of course, she really didn't have any right to provoke him like that, but his bid for her land had been so totally unexpected. And if she really wanted to be honest with herself, seeing him again had placed her completely on edge. Diana had never been too comfortable around men, and Chase Winfield represented something very disturbing. He had become, over the past few years, a unique, romantic memory. Perhaps because she knew she would never meet the wealthy, mysterious playboy whom she had rescued from the murky waters, the entire incident had evolved into a treasured fantasy. After all, the darkly handsome man in the tuxedo had called her beautiful. She had not even spoken a word to him while in the lake, and he had still desired her. The man in her recollections had been incredibly masterful, yet strangely tender. But the man of five years ago had also been drunk. His inhibitions had been completely broken down by alcohol. Yesterday the real man had returned, along with the inhibitions.

The poetic, passionate maniac from that fateful night no longer existed. At sixteen Diana had been given a glimpse of a side of the tycoon's character it was unlikely many other people had seen. Why couldn't she just forget it?

She turned out of the dirt driveway and onto Old Lake Road, practically colliding with a long yellow truck. It whizzed by her, the sound almost deafening, and she had barely enough time to read the logo on the side. A moving company! No need to know where *that* van was going. She put her foot down heavily on the gas pedal and headed into the village center.

Main Street on a Saturday morning was relatively crowded because this was the day everyone caught up on gossip, had the time to have a few drinks with old friends, and just, in general, socialize. Pete's old pickup was parked right outside the grocery.

"Little Di!" cried Manny from his traditional deck chair. "So you're finally gonna do it today?"

How mortifying, she thought. The entire village knew how badly the house needed a paint job. But she smiled back sheepishly. "Yeah, today's the day, Uncle Manny." He shook his balding head with a grin and watched her disappear inside the grocery store.

As usual, Myra, the proprietress, was holding court behind the postal window. All the regulars were there of course. They all greeted the newcomer with varying degrees of cordiality.

"I want to hear *all* about your new neighbor, Diana dear," gushed Mrs. Schuyler. "I'm sure he'd be just perfect for my Helga."

"Some men prefer brunettes to blondes, Katrina," remarked Myra, winking at Diana.

"And why wouldn't he like Helga?" objected Mrs. Schuyler.

"I never said he wouldn't *like* her, just that he might like a dark-haired girl better."

"Nonsense!" Katrina Schuyler made one of her broad gestures. "Helga—and I'm not just saying it because she's my own child—Helga looks like a goddess!"

Oh, no, here we go again, groaned Diana to herself. *Next we're going to have to hear the beauty pageant story.*

"I know for a fact she would have been Miss New York State if it hadn't been for that sprained index finger keeping her from winning the talent competition!"

In a way Diana felt somewhat sorry for the beautiful Helga: The poor girl's mother never left her alone.

"But, hey! Look who's here!" declared Willy Sutherland, deftly changing the subject. "I hope you remember to save me a dance, little lady."

"Willy," Diana sighed, "the Harvest Ball isn't for another three weeks."

"Sure, honey," replied the sprightly little gentleman. "But I always like to fill my dance card up in advance!"

The Harvest Ball had been a tradition in Silverwood Lake for over two hundred years, and there was no other occasion looked forward to with as much delight and eager anticipation. It was an occasion to celebrate all the bounty and beauty of the land—the apples, the cheeses, the cream, the corn. If Diana closed her eyes, she could almost smell the pumpkin pies and apple cobblers lined up along the refreshment tables in tempting array. Women planned their gowns for the ball far in advance. Most people attended the affair in period costume—lace and gingham and other finery of an era gone by. For true status this entailed a thorough search of the trunks in one's own attic. A brand new outfit designed by the poshest costume house in New York City would hardly evoke the same effect as a dress one could claim belonged to my great-grandmother." The older the better, was the motto at the Harvest Ball, an enchanted evening once every year, when time stood still.

"Myra," she said, changing the subject. "I'm going to need about seven gallons of white exterior."

"Oh?" The older woman smiled. "This could be a historic event! Did you hear that, everybody? Diana Mueller is taking the plunge at last!"

"Hallelujah," interjected Pete. "And make sure you give her the latex instead of the oil base, Myra."

"Your dear mother, Linette, God rest her soul, would be pleased," observed Katrina Schuyler. "Particularly if you took the trouble to give the house two coats."

I really need this, Diana mused silently. *I don't have enough aggravation already!*

"Don't forget to pick up your packet of tickets," Myra added.

Diana nodded. Except for her time away at college, she had gone with her mother each year to personally distribute the ball tickets. Their territory included the entire lakefront, just as the Schuylers' territory covered most of the south farm district. For the past two years Pete had graciously taken Linette Mueller's place. But now that Diana had come home at last, she would resume her old duties on the Harvest Ball ticket committee.

"Just wait till you hear about the fabulous door prize!" announced Willy.

"I'll help you with these cans," said Pete, following Myra and Diana to the hardware section of the cluttered store.

"How much is this going to cost?" asked Diana, watching with some concern as Myra furiously began pressing the keys of her pocket calculator. Money was tight for Diana these days. Even though the house had been paid off years ago, she still had to worry about monthly car payments and a rather hefty student loan.

"I'll let you know in a minute," said the proprietress.

Pete rubbed the gray stubble on his broad chin. "Now, see here, Myra, don't forget to give her ten percent discount for buying in volume."

The woman froze and stared up at him in an

extremely offended manner. "Are you insinuating, Peter Henry Turner, that I would knowingly cheat a customer?"

"Not in a million years," retorted Pete loftily. It was well understood that the man loved nothing better than getting under Myra MacPhee's skin. Perhaps one day he'd finally ask her to marry him.

Pete insisted that they load the heavy cans in the back of his own truck instead of the Chevy wagon. "You know, honey," he added, "you shouldn't have carried that ladder all by yourself yesterday."

"I didn't," she replied blandly.

"Oh?"

"Chase Winfield, uh, happened by and helped me."

Pete's eyebrows arched. "Fascinating. Tell me more."

"Oh, there's nothing much to tell. He didn't recognize me, thank goodness."

"I didn't expect he would, Diana," the older man reflected. "What's really bothering you?"

"We didn't exactly part amicably, Pete." She sighed. "I'm worried."

"So you'll kiss and make up!" her friend teased.

Diana shook her head forcefully. "It's not that at all." She paused. "Pete, why do you think he bought Grey Lodge?"

He shrugged, and continued to load the containers of paint. "I suppose everyone needs a place to get away to."

"So that's what you think, like everybody else in

town, that he bought it as a vacation home? I wish I could believe that."

He smiled. "Diana, Chase Winfield is not such a bad person. We had quite a pleasant talk that morning when he woke up on the sofa."

"That was five years ago," she scoffed. "Pete, he tried to buy my property yesterday."

He rubbed his hands together with relish. "I'm delighted to hear that, honey."

She stared at her friend in total puzzlement. "Why on earth would you be glad to hear something like that?"

"Because, Diana my dear, things were getting pretty dull around here." He slammed the tailgate with a flourish. "Now, maybe, they'll start to liven up some!"

Only optimistic old Pete would manage to see the bright side of a prospective land war, Diana mused later as she worked on the house front with her roller. She stood back and scrutinized the results of the past four hours. Not bad, not bad at all. The fresh white coat gleamed in the afternoon sunshine, and the distinctive paint smell filled her nostrils. She took a short break and drank some water. Taking the trouble to fix a sandwich was something she could well do without, especially with all that sticky paint that had somehow wedged itself underneath her fingernails. For a nurse, she certainly had poor eating habits. She would make it up to herself with a healthy, hot dinner this evening. Maybe she'd even dine by candlelight. After all, it was Saturday night!

The sun was sinking past the horizon when Diana finally decided to call it quits for the day. It wasn't the most careful paint job in the world, but if she rose early enough tomorrow, and worked until dusk, she could probably get the rest of the house done, not counting the shutters. For now, though, she'd better rinse off the roller and brushes so they wouldn't be stiff and useless in the morning.

She put everything in a large pail and trudged down, past the bushes, to the lake. It occurred to her that she was doing a bit of polluting on her own, and with a frustrated sigh she flung the pail back on the beach. She'd only rinse off the roller, and, of course, herself. To be sure, she was quite a sight. There was paint encrusted in her hair, smeared on her face, and splattered up and down her slim arms. Diana rolled up the legs of her overalls, kicked off her sneakers and striped socks, and waded into the water. She dragged the roller through the cool shallows until a cloudy whiteness tinted everything around her for a brief moment.

A nearby drone began to grow louder. Diana looked up and saw the sleek, shiny motorboat that had been moored at Grey Lodge. It slowed down and came to a stop about twenty feet away.

"I see that you're taking my advice," declared Chase Winfield from behind dark aviator sunglasses.

"I beg your pardon?" Diana replied, unnerved by his unexpected appearance, and more than slightly embarrassed by her own.

"Obviously, you've undertaken quite a paint

job," he remarked, motioning to her white-splattered hair, body, and clothing. "Painting your house will certainly increase its market value."

"I'm not interested in increasing the market value," Diana uttered defiantly. "It's not a chunk of real estate, it's a home. *My* home."

"What are you?" inquired Chase Winfield, pulling off his sunglasses and scrutinizing her in the fading sunlight. "Seventeen, eighteen years old?"

"Twenty-one." She crossed her arms and took several steps toward him until the water was up to the middle of her thigh. "I'm not some little kid, as you apparently believe."

He smiled thinly. "You hardly look your age, Diana." There was a pause. "Did you tell your parents about my offer?"

"They're both dead, Mr. Winfield. It's my home, as I've already told you."

The hardness of his face seemed to soften slightly. "So, you live here all by yourself?"

"Yes." Diana cast her eyes downward for a moment.

"What kind of a life is that for a young girl?" He asked curiously. "It must get terribly lonesome for you out here."

Did she detect a note of sympathy in his voice? No, that was impossible. And anyhow, the last thing she wanted was anyone, particularly Chase Winfield, feeling sorry for her. She'd never admit in a thousand years how lonesome it sometimes was for her. "Not at all, Mr. Winfield. We here at Silverwood Lake treasure our privacy."

"And what do you do on a typical Saturday night?" he ventured casually. "Or is this some indication?" There was a slightly deprecatory nod in the direction of her dripping overalls and paint roller.

"That's hardly any of your affair, Mr. Winfield!" she snapped back.

"If you call me *Mr.* Winfield one more time, I'll personally come over there and dunk your head underwater!"

Diana stared at him in momentary disbelief. Did this man actually possess a sense of humor? Her own lips twitched.

"What's this?" he suddenly remarked with amusement. "Are you almost smiling?" All at once there was another long pause. "I know this will probably sound crazy, Diana, but have we ever met before?"

"I don't see how," she answered quickly.

He seemed puzzled, but only for a moment. "By the way, how is this lake for swimming?"

Diana cleared her throat hastily. "As you can see, it's crystal-clear, Mr. Win—Chase."

He nodded approvingly. "I'll have to give it a try sometime before it gets too chilly." And then, as if he had difficulty finding the right words, he finally said, "About yesterday . . ."

"It was my fault," Diana interrupted. "I was unnecessarily rude."

"*I* was the one who was rude," Chase insisted firmly.

"Why don't we just say we were both rude and leave it at that?" she suggested with a smile.

He nodded, and even at a distance she was aware of a sparkle in his eyes. With his black hair all windblown, and the tight-fitting navy polo shirt setting off his tanned, muscular arms, he was decidedly attractive sitting there at the wheel of his boat. So male, so healthy.

"Are you really twenty-one?" he asked with a slight tone of disbelief.

"Now you *are* the one who is definitely being rude!" Diana pulled the roller from the lake and began shaking the water out of it.

He watched the simple motion thoughtfully. "Most women would consider that a compliment." He turned on the engine again, and, after giving her a wave, he steered the craft away.

Diana waited until the motorboat retreated into the distance, and began to wade ashore. For some strange reason she found it slightly disheartening that Chase Winfield had mistaken her for a teenager. Later that evening, before stepping into the shower, she surveyed her reflection in the mirror. Admittedly, with her hair in pigtails and the baggy cotton overalls, she didn't exactly look like a woman of the world. A few years down the road she would probably be grateful to look younger than she was. She stripped off her clothes and pulled out the ponytail clips. She clinically examined the image in the looking glass. Her body was smooth, supple, and quite shapely. She certainly had the figure of a young woman.

It must get terribly lonesome for you. He had said to her. How right, how very right the man was.

She turned on the faucets full force and stepped into the stall, shutting the glass door behind her. Ducking her head under the powerful spray, she let the steamy jet saturate her hair and neck. She reached for the baby shampoo and massaged some into her scalp until it lathered up fully. The dilemma faced by herself and Helga, even Sara Lee Hutchins, was not unusual in small towns. A woman loved her home, the place where she had been born and raised. And if you were fortunate enough to find a job you enjoyed there, why would you ever choose to leave? Well, she didn't *want* to leave Silverwood Lake. She loved it here. If there were only a person to share it with. But it was becoming more obvious, that if she was searching for love, she wasn't going to find it in this remote village. Just from sheer logistics the odds were strongly against such an occurrence. Sooner or later she would have to venture into what was laughingly called "the real world." A larger town. A city perhaps. Every instinct within her cried out against such a move, but facts were facts. The years would go by, and she would become lonelier and lonelier, and then what? Would she end up bound to her house, an aging spinster?

Quickly, she chased the picture from her mind. This was all conjecture, all worrisome nonsense. She was young; she had all the time in the world. And anyhow, who said that a woman had to be married? She squeezed the excess water from her hair defiantly. Who said that a woman had to go hunting for a man? Diana sighed. The real dream, the true fantasy, was to have love find *her*. In the old days it was the man, after all, who did the hunting. What had happened in recent times to change the image of women into a species of pursuers, chasing down their elusive prey? It irritated her to remember that her own namesake, Diana, conjured up a picture of that legendary Olympian goddess, a ruthless Amazon with her bows and arrows and pack of vicious hunting dogs. But Diana the Huntress had turned away from love many times. In fact, she had remained true to her eternal vow of chastity.

Diana of the present stepped out of the shower and wrapped herself in a fluffy old towel. Speaking of chastity, she was following the mythological pattern herself. At twenty-one, she was still a virgin, a rather rare state of affairs if her girlfriends at college were any indication. But her upbringing had been rather strict, and besides, it wasn't as if many opportunities had presented themselves.

She wrapped a smaller towel around her head. Why not be honest? Ever since that night at the lake, five years ago, she had compared every boy she met to Chase Winfield, and they paled by comparison. And now, out of the blue, the man had returned to Silverwood Lake. Of course, for how long, and, ultimately, for what purpose, she had no true way of knowing. Not yet, anyhow. The only thing she *did* know, was that Chase Winfield was increasingly beginning to resemble the man in her memories, a memory she had hoped was buried at last. He would never know what had really transpired that fateful September night, but to Diana the irony of it all was almost too much to believe. He had been the hunter. She had been his prey. And now the hunter was back.

Chapter Four

Monday was easily the worst day in the week. In the first place, every muscle in Diana's weary body still ached from the exertions of her weekend painting marathon. Secondly, Dr. Myers had been called away on a medical emergency in Greenfield and had left Diana in charge of the clinic. On a normal morning this situation would have been difficult enough to handle, but this particular morning marked the first day of innoculations for the coming school year. The tiny waiting area was jammed with wailing kindergartners who clung anxiously to their mothers and tearfully awaited their turn behind the screen.

Right now she was having serious trouble trying to convince little Bobby Wyler that a measles vaccine would only take a minute.

"I don' wanna!" The five-year-old struggled in her arms.

"Now, you see here, Bobby," boomed Mrs. Wyler from across the room, where she sat holding the twins, age six months. "You let Nurse Diana give you that shot, or I'll come right over there and smack your bottom!"

"But it'll hurt!" he whimpered at Diana.

She set him down on the table and whispered confidentially. "It hurts only for one bitty second. Even Batman says so."

"Does *he* get one?" The little boy's eyes grew as large as saucers.

Diana dabbed at a small portion of his skin with a piece of absorbent cotton, and readied the needle. "You bet he does, Bobby. He comes in here once a year!" Within a matter of seconds she had dispatched the injection and little Bobby Wyler, who was forced to admit that it wasn't that bad anyhow.

"Was I as brave as Batman?"

Diana smiled and handed him a lollipop. "You bet!" Well, at least the children weren't afraid of her. She glanced at the mirror by the drug cabinet. In the crisp white dress, light stockings, and her hair pulled back in a neat ponytail, her appearance was not what one would call formidable. By the time she innoculated the last child, though, she was looking forward to a little peace and quiet.

"There, there," she soothed two-year-old Ramona Johnson, who sobbed loudly enough to be heard all over a sports arena. "It'll be all right," she assured the tiny girl gently before emerging from behind the screen. "You'll be all right now."

There was no way she could have been aware that barely a moment before, a tall, lean man had entered the clinic and stood patiently in the waiting area, only a few yards from the screened-off section. He was dressed in jeans and a well-cut tattersall shirt, which was rolled up at the sleeves. A long, jagged cut began at the elbow and ended at the base of one wrist. Just as little Ramona Johnson began to wail at the top of her lungs at the moment of her vaccination, he shook his head wryly, recalling his own childhood. And then he heard the gentle, comforting voice behind the screen, and something seemed to go *ping* in the back of his brain. There was something vaguely familiar about the words, something oddly reminiscent. A dream, half remembered. Chase Winfield chided himself for being sentimental. It had to be his mind playing tricks on him, or just mark it down to an overactive imagination.

"You'll be all right now. . . ." No, it wasn't his imagination. He had heard those words before, spoken in exactly that way. It certainly hadn't been his mother, or a kindly maiden aunt, because he had never known either. The memory was far more recent. And he knew very well the dream it came from. It was that same wonderful dream he'd been having on and off for the past five years, although, for the past several days, he'd be having it each time he went to sleep. Strange. Why couldn't he put it all together? Why did there always seem to be a piece missing?

Diana handed the toddler back to her mother, and they emerged from behind the screen. There, to her amazement, stood Chase Winfield, who stared at her in apparent confusion.

"You're the nurse?" he inquired, his voice colored with surprise.

She smiled. "Don't look so astonished, Mr. Winfield." Mrs. Johnson and child left the room, virtually unnoticed.

Chase Winfield's eyes traveled slowly over her body, taking in the well-fitting, short white uniform. "You make a very pretty nurse."

Two bright spots of pink appeared on Diana's cheeks. The compliment had been so totally unexpected that for a second she was completely flustered. What saved her from being reduced to a stammering schoolgirl was the fact that at precisely that moment, she noticed the ugly cut on his arm.

"What happened to you?" she exclaimed, immediately reaching out to examine his arm.

Chase Winfield was still regarding her with a puzzled expression, as if he had just walked into the center of a hurricane. Almost mechanically, he stretched out the injured limb for her inspection. "It's only a scratch; you really don't have to bother. What I really wanted was a tetanus shot."

Diana touched the firm flesh of his tanned forearm. The warm, hard feel of him gave her a definitely unprofessional tingle. "Have you had a shot recently?"

Chase Winfield didn't take his eyes off her face. He was studying her intently. "What?"

"I asked when the last time was that you had a tetanus shot."

He shrugged. "It's been years. I have no idea, actually."

Diana reached for the antiseptic. "First, we'd better clean this."

"All I need is the shot," he protested.

"Oh, and when did you get your R.N. degree, Mr. Winfield?"

He sighed. "It's Chase. How many times do I have to tell you?"

"All right, Chase. Why don't you sit over on that table? It'll be easier for me to work that way."

He followed her to the screened-off area, and, pausing just a moment, hoisted himself up on the table. Silently, he watched as she finished cleaning the ugly cut, and applied several butterfly bandage strips to help aid the healing.

"You've been a very good little boy," she declared in her most professional manner. "What flavor lollipop would you like?"

His mouth opened slightly in amusement, then shut again.

"All good little children get lollipops here. Don't be shy!" She was surprising even herself at the cavalier way she was speaking to him, but somehow, in the clinic, behind the protection of the uniform, it seemed rather safe.

"I'm not shy," he finally answered quietly. "On the other hand, I honestly can't say that I've been *good.*"

Diana nervously stepped over to the cabinet. "So, tell me," she tried to change the subject quickly. "How did you cut yourself?"

"It was pretty stupid, actually," he admitted. "I was rewiring in the library and managed to scrape my arm with a piece of scrap metal."

Diana returned with a disposable syringe. "Roll up your other sleeve a little higher, please."

Silently, Chase obliged. He didn't even wince when she administered the injection, but the moment she removed the needle and pressed down on the flesh with a piece of absorbent cotton, he looked up at her. "What perfume are you wearing?"

"I'm not wearing any perfume," she answered with a slight quiver. Why would he think she was wearing perfume? Besides, how could anyone smell anything in this room except the overpowering aroma of rubbing alcohol and liniment?

She removed the cotton ball and replaced it with a tiny, round Band-Aid. The action brought her face almost in direct contact with his. Quickly, she bent her head, and this gesture caused several wisps of hair to brush along the bare skin of his neck.

"Are you sure you're not wearing any perfume?" he repeated softly.

"Just soap and water," she replied, unable to

understand why her stomach was suddenly doing somersaults. There was something so very intimate about the moment, and it had only a little to do with the fact that he was hovering so closely above her on the examining table. Or the fact that they were together behind the screen, and alone in the clinic. There was a shattering intimacy about his words.

"Soap and water smells delightful on you, Diana." His silvery eyes glittered into hers. "I believe I'll have that lollipop now."

"What flavor?" she inquired, striving to keep her voice normal.

"Flavor?" he repeated, his gaze slowly traveling to her lips. Odd, why hadn't he noticed until this minute how soft and pink her mouth looked. "Why don't you pick a flavor for me, Diana? Something . . . sweet."

The subtle hint of sensuality in his reply completely eluded Diana. "They're all sweet," she said, reaching for the little straw candy basket. "I'm partial to root beer." She handed him a tiny cellophane-wrapped amber lollipop. He took it from her and slipped it into his shirt pocket.

"On second thought, I'll save this for later." There was a long pause, almost as if he were sitting there, waiting for her to say something.

She felt unusually self-conscious, and brushed a loose strand of brown hair out of her eyes. "That's all, Mr. Win—Chase. You can stand up now." With an attempt at briskness she walked away from the table and over toward the main counter.

"Thank you, Nurse Diana." His voice followed her, and in another minute he was casually leaning over the counter, rolling down both sleeves. "What's the damage?"

"I beg your pardon?"

"What do I owe you for services rendered?" His mouth wrinkled up in one corner.

"Oh." Diana pulled out a clipboard with carbon sheets. "That's seven dollars for the shot. You can pay by cash or check."

His eyes sparkled. Funny, she'd never noticed the wonderful laugh lines before. "I believe you've forgotten something."

She held her pen midair. "What?"

"Your wonderful bandaging effort on my arm, Nurse Diana."

Diana shrugged. "Forget it." She continued to fill out the receipt.

Chase stilled her arm. "Wait. I'm serious, Diana. You can't run a business this way."

She set down her pen. "This isn't a business, it's a health-care facility."

He shook his head determinedly. "Whatever. You can't keep this little enterprise running in the black if you don't maintain proper fees."

Diana's mouth tightened. "Are you telling me how to do my job, Chase Winfield?"

He inclined his dark head. "I'm just telling you that when a patient like me can obviously afford to pay his way, then you should make sure he does."

Diana tossed the clipboard across the counter. "Oh, honestly!"

He ignored her irritation. "Now, if I were back in the city, and received these equivalent services in my doctor's office, I would expect to pay at least forty or fifty dollars." He reached into the back pocket of his jeans and pulled out a black leather wallet. He removed several fifty-dollar bills and placed them down on the laminated counter.

She glanced down at the crisp green notes with a mixture of embarrassment and disdain. "We don't need your charity!"

"Indeed?" came the cool reply. "You seemed to think that *I* needed *yours.*"

Diana's eyes blazed. "Oh, just forget it! Forget I even try to be nice to you, Chase Winfield."

"Now, how could I forget something like that?" His gaze was enigmatic. "You have the gentlest touch of any nurse I know, but the fact remains that as your patient, I should be offering adequate compensation for your services." There was a long pause. "Are you going to become all proud and huffy and insist, very stupidly, that this clinic can't use all the extra money it can get?"

She folded her arms. "Of course we can, but—"

He pushed the money toward her. "I'm not used to arguing about trivial matters like this, Diana."

"I daresay you aren't." Goodness, why was she making such a fuss over his generosity? The truth was, the clinic really did need that extra hundred and fifty dollars. There was all that new testing equipment that Dr. Myers had his eye on these days. And there was the matter of the new children's infirmary that was still waiting in vain to be built.

She wanted to say thank-you to Chase Winfield, but a contrary imp of pride was still paralyzing her tongue. Maybe it was because she had attempted to treat him like anyone else in Silverwood Lake and he had blatantly reminded her that he was Mr. Millionaire. Oh, not exactly. She was reading too much into his actions, but the fact was, he could never be just another resident of the village.

"I was only trying to treat you the same way I'd treat anyone else around here." Unconsciously, she had spoken the words aloud.

His hard face appeared to actually soften. "I believe you were, Diana. I truly believe you were. Thank you for that." There was a long, drawn-out silence, and then, without another word, he turned and left the clinic.

Diana could only stare after him in bewilderment. What had just happened between them? Something *had* happened, and it wasn't her imagination. Despite all she had heard about the aloof Chase Winfield, for just a few moments he had not been aloof with her. But the odd part of it was that she still knew no more about him now than she had five years ago. The aura of mystery continued to surround him. Why would a multimillionaire purchase such a rundown old house and insist on doing the rewiring himself? And here it was, already Monday.

How could he seclude himself here, away from his numerous business enterprises, for so long? According to Myra MacPhee, the phones at Grey Lodge hadn't even been turned on yet. What was really going on?

Diana picked up the three fifty-dollar bills and folded them into the metal cash box. Well, it was probably none of her business, anyhow. She glanced around the empty room vaguely, and decided she'd best take advantage of the lull in activity by reorganizing the patient file. The only clerical help they could afford at the clinic were the volunteers from the local Red Cross chapter who came in on weekends.

Fortunately, the proceeds from this year's Harvest Ball were earmarked for the clinic fund. At five dollars a person, they could raise several thousand dollars, not counting the bonus raffle.

But she'd forgotten completely about the tickets! In all her preoccupation with painting the house this past weekend, she'd totally neglected to distribute her share of the ball tickets. Even though the ball was nearly three weeks away, it was only proper courtesy to deliver them to the residents in her area well in advance. No doubt Helga Schuyler and her mother had practically finished their territory by now.

Diana sighed guiltily as she remembered the still-unopened packet of gold-edged invitations resting on her kitchen table. Every year Willy Suterland had them specially printed at no charge by his cousin in Rochester who owned a stationery company.

It occurred to her that one of the people on her list included the lake's newest resident. Diana was rather skeptical concerning his attendance at such an event. Of course, she could be wrong, but Chase Winfield did not seem like the type who frequented rural dances. From all she had read about him in the personality magazines, he seemed more inclined to nightclubs and cocktail parties. If he supported a charity, the bashes he appeared at were most likely to be in the poshest hotels in New York City or San Francisco. Probably, the closest he ever had come to a rural social setting was a summer cotillion at one of those exclusive country clubs reserved strictly for bluebloods whose yearly incomes exceeded one million dollars.

Maybe she was being fanciful nonetheless. The man had given no indication that he was even remotely interested in becoming part of the local social scene. Yes, it was possible that she was misjudging Chase Winfield.

She slammed the metal file drawer shut. It was also possible that she was spending altogether too much time wondering about Chase Winfield and his various activities. What did it matter to her what the man did? She recalled the odd sensation in her stomach when he'd suddenly questioned her about the perfume she certainly *wasn't* wearing. And how could she possibly forget when out of the clear blue sky he had called her pretty?

Of course, it would be wise not to read too much into it. Even with her lack of experience, she knew enough about men to be aware that they paid compliments like that quite frequently. There was nothing personal about them. She'd really be deluding herself if she believed for even one moment that Chase Winfield had actually been attempting to flirt with her. The very idea was absurd! She glanced at her wristwatch. The shift ended at three o'clock. That would give her at least three good hours of sunlight to cover a large portion of the lake and its surrounding woods. She could probably distribute twenty-five or even thirty tickets in that time.

Diana busied herself with the duties in the clinic, but more than once during the afternoon her thoughts returned to Chase and the puzzled expression on his face the moment she had emerged from behind the screen with Ramona Johnson. For a moment she could have sworn he actually appeared flustered. Most probably, this was yet another example of her overactive imagination. She'd really have to do something about *that.*

At precisely three o'clock Diana was able to leave work on time because, for once, Dr. Myers had returned to close up. She drove home quickly, and changed from her white uniform into the far more comfortable jeans and T-shirt. Even at three-thirty the sun still shone brightly above the lake, and a comfortable breeze blew warm and moist with the rich flavor of Indian summer. She trudged along the underbrush to her first stop, Pete Turner's cottage.

He was dozing comfortably on a hammock stretched between two very old, very strong elm trees, with an equally comfortable old Hans dozing at his feet. They both looked like something out of Rip Van Winkle. Diana smiled to herself, and pulled out a card with MR. PETER TURNER handwritten in the elegant, spidery script of Mavis Gumbler, perennial chairwoman of the Harvest Ball committee. Mavis was nearly ninety years old and just as much a Silverwood institution as the ball itself. Rumor had it that Mavis had given her heart only once, to a boy who had been killed in France during World War I. Diana tried to picture the now-wrinkled, fragile old spinster as she must have looked during her youth, dancing at the Harvest Ball with her beau. She supposed such moments were forever frozen in time for Mavis.

Diana sometimes wondered if she had been born too late. Maybe she herself belonged in a more romantic era, where women wore bustles and lace, and men knew how to court a lady. The sound of Pete's snoring brought her back to the present. She cleared her throat loudly and began to read the card.

"Mr. Peter Turner, on behalf of the Harvest Ball committee, you are most cordially requested to attend our annual gala and join us in the joyous festivities at the usual place and the usual time on the last Saturday in the month of September—" She paused. Was Pete even beginning to stir?

"Well, go on!" a voice growled. "Finish inviting me!"

"I thought so," she declared. "Pretending to be asleep again!"

Pete yawned and grinned up at her. "No, don't go on. I'd rather not know what the raffle prize is this year."

Diana handed him the invitation. "Grand prize is a portable television set; first prize is a Christmas turkey."

Her old friend shrugged. "I'd rather have the turkey."

"I'm not surprised." She glanced absently at the sleeping Hans. "He's tired these days, isn't he?"

Pete sighed, and rubbed the animal's neck affectionately. "He's getting old, honey. I guess we both are."

"Oh, you're not getting old!" she protested.

"Don't try to be tactful, honey. I'm a lot older now than I was a year ago. Not that I'm ready to shuffle off or anything but—" He paused. "I did get a very substantial offer today."

Diana cocked her head curiously. "What kind of offer?"

Pete continued to rock in the threadbare hammock, his plump arms now resting beneath his graying head. "Somebody was willing to take this little half acre off my hands. He was willing to pay a small fortune for it, too."

Diana bit her lower lip. "Need I ask who that somebody was?"

Pete gave another indifferent shrug. "Naturally, I

told our mutual acquaintance, Mr. Winfield, that I wasn't at all interested."

"Did he take no for an answer?"

The old man stifled another yawn. "Strangely enough, he didn't press the issue. On the other hand, he had better luck with our other neighbors."

A muscle suddenly constricted in Diana's throat. Finally, she managed to say, "What do you mean?"

"I mean, honey, you'll find out soon enough when you go over there to deliver their invitations. Johann and Gretchen Reiss, and most probably, the Bergers, too."

Diana couldn't believe it. "They sold out?"

Pete sat up and the hammock rocked crazily with the shift in weight. "I'm not really surprised. Things haven't been going that well for Johann since Gretchen got ill. He's really wanted to move her down to a warmer climate."

"But they were both *born* here!" Diana protested. "And the Bergers—"

"Johann's brother has a place in St. Petersburg that he's been offering to share for years. And as far as the Bergers are concerned, now Fred has enough money for a down payment on that small tavern in Greenfield. We both know that's what he's always wanted. He never thought he'd be able to afford it."

Diana adjusted the packet of invitations under her arm and shifted her weight restlessly. "I don't like this at all, Pete. Not at all."

The older man smiled. "Honey, you can't blame

people for wanting something better than they have."

"I know, I know. It's just that it's all happening so fast. Too fast." She scratched her head. "Chase Winfield has descended upon us like a tornado. What's next, I wonder?"

Pete rose to his feet and thrust his brawny hands into the pockets of his worn trousers. "Perhaps you should have asked 'Who's next?' "

Pete certainly was right, she thought an hour later, having delivered ten other invitations. While at the Berger household, she had been struck by the unusual air of excitement that seemed to infect the entire family. Lola Berger's face was a picture of sheer happiness.

"Oh, Diana!" she exclaimed, reaching into her purse to pay for her ball tickets. "It's like a dream come true!" Radiantly, she turned to her husband. "Isn't that so, dearie?"

"That's what it is," Fred Berger beamed back, "a dream come true!"

"Can you just imagine that wonderful Mr. Winfield? Offering us nearly two hundred thousand dollars for just this broken-down house, and telling us we could still live in it as long as it took us to get settled in Greenfield. He even said he'd help us find a place if we had any trouble." Lola took her husband's hand. "Isn't that Mr. Winfield just marvelous?"

Diana nodded mutely. She felt an odd sense of

loss, and the slightest inkling of betrayal. The Bergers were actually pulling up stakes and leaving. Of course, she could understand that the offer had been too tempting to refuse, and she certainly didn't want to put a damper on their obvious happiness.

The scene was pretty much the same at the Reiss home.

"The winters were getting so harsh for Mama," declared Johann, "and we've both always loved Florida."

Diana smiled sadly. She would truly miss the kindly old couple. What would life on the lake be like without the Reisses? Still, she had to admit that Johann seemed like a man who had just had a heavy burden lifted from his shoulders.

"Our worries are over," added Gretchen. "You would not believe, Diana, what Mr. Winfield is willing to pay for this property. You simply would not believe it! Perhaps he is a madman." She clasped her frail hands together. "Or maybe just a fool."

Diana was still shaking her head in disbelief as she continued her trek around the lake. Some neighbors hadn't arrived home from work yet, but those who were there to pay for their tickets all had comments concerning Chase Winfield's recent actions. Some people had strong opinions in one direction; they would never, under any circumstances, sell their property. In most cases, the land had been in the same family for generations.

"He's one of them industrialists, Diana. I've seen

what they do," commented Frank Ramsey. "They buy up a whole town, and the next thing you know it's one big airplane runway!"

On the other hand, there were many other people like the Reisses and the Bergers, who were seriously considering Chase's offers. For some, the specter of unemployment loomed large on the horizon; for other, younger residents, the isolation of the community had become just too much in recent years.

"What would you do if *you* were widowed, with two little children?" demanded Anna Smith, an attractive woman in her early thirties who was finding the loneliness more than she could bear. "I'll never meet a man here, Diana. It's hard enough for someone like you, who's young, and doesn't have any kids. The cards are really stacked up against me here. If Chase Winfield makes me a decent offer for my house, I'll jump at it."

Well, Diana reflected later, staring out on the glittering blue lake, she couldn't really blame someone like Anna for wanting to make a new start. She couldn't blame any of her neighbors. Still, it was a frightening sensation to feel as if one were on a sinking ship, with all the passengers and crew abandoning it. If only she knew what the new captain had in mind. *Why* was Chase so eagerly grabbing up all the property that he could? What was behind it? She had a distinctly uncomfortable premonition about his motives. They did not bode anything pleasant for the future of Silverwood Lake, that was certain. She squinted, and stared across the water toward the setting sun. There was still some time left to make one more delivery, and she'd been putting this particular one off for long enough.

Grey Lodge was set on thirty secluded acres, only three of which fronted the lake. The rest of the property fanned out into the surrounding woods, and framed the rambling Victorian structure. She approached the front of the spacious home, which boasted a broad expanse of lush green lawn. Years ago the Greys had installed an underground sprinkler system. But it had been a long time since anyone had trimmed the grass. It rustled softly in the breeze, gently caressing Diana's jean-clad legs. She paused and regarded the quietness in the air. If it weren't for the blue Mercedes sedan in the driveway, Diana might have thought that no one was home.

Cautiously, she approached the huge oak front door, with its delicate stained-glass fanlight. With the diamond-paned windows still intact after all these years, she was forced to admit that Grey Lodge was one of the loveliest homes she had ever seen. There was something special about the place. Of course, she thought with a smirk, Chase Winfield had been in no position to tell *her* about her house needing a paint job. She idly observed the peeling front portico. Yes, it was a most beautiful home, but sadly in need of some loving attention. With a feeling of apprehension she rang the doorbell.

After several minutes she rang again. There was no answer. Well, perhaps no one was home after all.

In a way, she felt strangely relieved. Just as she was about to take the invitation marked MR. CHASE WINFIELD and stuff it back into the manila envelope, the front door suddenly flew open. Towering over her in surprise was Chase, wearing only slacks, his muscular chest tanned and bare.

"Diana!" he exclaimed. "What are you doing here?"

She felt mortified, silently watching the man before her run a hand through his rumpled black hair, his eyes obviously drowsy with sleep.

"I've woken you up! I'm sorry!" She lowered her gaze to the floor and noticed that his feet, too, were bare.

"Oh, no, it's all right!" Chase replied quickly. "I was just about to get up anyway. You might say I keep very odd hours." With a half smile he held the door open wider, and stepped back to let her inside.

"Are you sure it's no trouble?" she asked with just the slightest trace of reluctance.

"Of course I'm sure! Come on in, neighbor."

She stepped inside slowly, and he shut the door behind her. They stood there in the dark center hall of the lodge. Diana had never been inside. It was all rather gloomy, the furniture covered in dust sheets, although there were many wooden crates in the center of the room marked WINFIELD ENTERPRISES, INC., CALIFORNIA.

Chase Winfield stared at her for another moment. The last person he expected to come knocking on his door was that adorable little Diana Mueller. The first couple of times he'd seen her, he remembered thinking that she was a cute kid even if she was a bit too sassy for her own good. Still, there was something about her that puzzled him, and he wasn't sure what it was. Maybe that strange feeling that he'd seen her someplace before. Of course, he dismissed that right away as being absolutely impossible. But today, the third time he met her, he realized that she wasn't just a kid. In that form-fitting white dress, and her hair pulled back in a glossy brown ponytail, she was a damn pretty young woman. Not spectacular in the way he was used to, but with a unique attraction of her own. He remembered the silky light stockings she had worn earlier in the day and smiled to himself. And those legs of hers weren't bad, either. If only he could figure out what was puzzling him about her. She seemed a little nervous now, standing restlessly in the hallway. Maybe he should toss a shirt on or something.

"Make yourself comfortable," he said suddenly. "I'll be back in a minute." Without waiting for her response he went swiftly into the next room, where his suitcase lay open on a chair. He reached for the top item in his pile of clothing, a plain white oxford-cloth shirt. Carelessly, he tugged it on and buttoned it in one hasty gesture.

He wondered what the girl could want. Normally, his ego would have permitted him to venture that she was paying him a social call, but from what he already knew of her, that seemed highly unlikely. He smiled again, this time more wryly. She was definitely adorable, and her attentions would be more than welcome, but it was quite obviously the furthest thing from the woman's mind. He slipped into a comfortable old pair of leather deck shoes. He recalled the way she had blushed today. When was the last time he had seen a woman blush? No woman he had ever known had ever blushed. There was something very refreshing about Diana Mueller's reaction to him, although, in the back of his mind, something still disturbed him.

She stood there in the exact same position he had left her in the hallway. She had a wrinkled manila envelope under her arm and a barely detectable expression of nervousness on her face. Ah, yes, it was most definitely business she had come to discuss. Chase gave an inward sigh of satisfaction. Most probably she had changed her mind about selling that ramshackle old house of hers. Good. A sweet young thing like her didn't deserve to be cooped up in a remote village like this. She belonged in the city where she could enjoy herself and meet people. Men, especially. Then Diana looked up at him with her huge amber eyes and he was, at once, inexplicably envious of the young men that she would soon be meeting in her new life in the city.

"Don't tell me," he murmured. "You've come to talk about my offer."

Diana almost choked. "Is that what you really think?" How very typical of the man! She should have expected he would assume such a logical reason for her unexpected visit.

"Of course, what else would bring you to my humble abode, neighbor?" This time there was just the slightest innuendo in his response, which she could not fail to miss. "And let me assure you, Diana," he continued confidently, "you won't regret this decision for a minute. With a substantial nest egg you could make quite a life for yourself in the city."

The unmitigated gall of him! Diana fumed inwardly but held her temper for the count of ten, just like her father had once taught her. She'd set this man straight in just another moment. He just stood there, blithely rolling up the sleeves of his expensive white shirt, so very sure of himself! She took another breath and then gave him her sweetest, most ladylike smile. Removing the gilt-edged card from her envelope, she read aloud, "Mr. Chase Winfield, on behalf of the Harvest Ball committee, you are most cordially requested to attend our annual gala and join us in the joyous festivities at the usual place and at the usual time on the last Saturday in the month of September, in the time-honored tradition of our wonderful community." There was a long silence, and Diana looked up. She almost burst out laughing when she saw the ludicrous expression on Chase's face. "And, oh, yes," she added, "the donation is five dollars payable to me, or at the door, should you choose to attend."

He shook his head. "You're inviting me to a dance?"

"The Harvest Ball committee is inviting you," she

corrected quickly. "Now that you're a resident, you're included in all local events. It's customary."

He thrust his hands into the pockets of his slacks. "I suppose I should say I'm touched."

"Are you?" There was a tinge of annoyance in her voice. "You sound more like you're amused by us."

"Oh, what gives you that idea?" His eyes crinkled down at her. "I've never been to . . . what would you call it? A barn raising—"

"It's not a barn raising," she countered brusquely. "It's just what the invitation says it is—a ball."

"I stand corrected," he replied with mock solemnity.

"I should have known you wouldn't be interested, but at least I thought you wouldn't poke fun at our traditions. This may not be Manhattan or San Francisco, but at least we have manners!" She turned on her heel and headed angrily for the door.

"Hey! Just a minute!" A strong arm shot out and gripped her shoulder. "A feisty little thing, aren't you?" His silvery gaze surveyed her own blazing eyes with amusement.

"You shouldn't be so touchy, you know."

"I wasn't being touchy!" Diana exclaimed, unable to pull back from the tight clasp of his hand on her slim shoulder. "But you, Chase Winfield, are a snob!"

Out of nowhere, his other hand settled down on Diana's left shoulder. "Quite a temper you've got, little Diana!" As he pulled her closer to him she could feel the warmth emanating from him. "How dare you accuse me of being a snob? Just, how dare you, tiger cat!" His head lowered toward hers until his mouth hovered barely inches from her own.

Diana gave a quick swallow. "Oh, yes! And one more thing," she added breathlessly. "The Harvest Ball committee is pleased to announce the prizes for this year's raffle, all proceeds to go to the clinic fund. . . ."

"Am I making you nervous?" Chase murmured silkily.

"Certainly not!" she lied. "Did you know that we're offering a wonderful grand prize for this year's drawing—a twelve-inch portable color television set, courtesy of Van Peer's Hardware and Appliance Emporium."

"Forget the raffle!" he whispered into her ear, his lips nearly brushing her tender lobe. "You're an adorable creature, Diana!" In one swift motion he pulled her slim body against his hard frame, and his mouth descended onto hers.

For just a split second Diana's lips remained still and unyielding against this unexpected assault. But suddenly, an intensely pleasurable sensation shot through her, straight down to her toes, and her mouth grew soft and responsive beneath his. Never in her life had she been kissed so thoroughly, so expertly. Chase gave a low groan of pleasure and let his hands travel down her shoulders till they reached her waist. He drew her even more tightly to him, and was just about to part her lips with his probing tongue when Diana gave a cry of protest and wrenched herself free from his grasp.

"I didn't come here for this!" she protested, astonished at the devastating impact of his kiss.

"No, I suppose you didn't." Chase put his hands back into his pockets and gazed at her enigmatically. "I assume you expect me to apologize for my . . . shall we say, boorish behavior just now?"

She shrugged nervously. "Forget it."

"Now *that's* something that's easier said than done." He sighed wearily. "Tell me something, Diana Mueller. Why do we always seem to provoke each other?"

She averted her eyes. "I—I honestly don't know." Her lips still tingled from the contact with his. A kiss from Chase Winfield had been the very last thing Diana had expected when she had shown up at Grey Lodge. On the other hand, at least subconsciously, she had always wondered what it would be like, the embrace of a man who had hovered in the shadow of her dreams for the past five years. Every time, at the precise moment he pulled her close and was about to kiss her, she had always awakened. But this time, this first time, it had been no dream. It had been reality, and she had not been torn from her sleep. The kiss, as brief as it was, had been everything she had imagined it could be. But she could never permit Chase Winfield to know it.

"How about some coffee, Diana?" he asked suddenly.

"Uh, no thanks. I've got to get going." She smiled uncomfortably, and tucked her T-shirt more tightly back into the waistband of her dungarees. Somehow, it must have come loose during that startling embrace.

He took a few steps in her direction. "What's your hurry?"

A flush tinted her face. "I've . . . that is, there are still other invitations I ought to be delivering."

His mouth thinned. "Why do I get the impression you're not being altogether honest with me, Diana?"

Damn him, she thought. On top of everything else, he's a mindreader, too! "No, really," she insisted, holding out the manila envelope as proof. "There are at least twenty more cards in here." Cards which she very well knew she had no intention of distributing until tomorrow. It was almost dark by now.

"Were you actually intending to deliver all of them tonight?" he replied doubtfully.

"I'd better be on my way while there's still some sun."

"Diana." There was a troubled note in his voice. "Have I frightened you away?" He reached out his hand and ran a single finger across her cheek and down the silky length of her ponytail.

"Of course not," she said, unable to suppress a slight quiver at his touch.

"About what just happened," Chase's gaze lingered silver-gray on her face. "I simply couldn't resist."

"Yes," she retorted. "I'm sure you were merely being neighborly!" Naturally, she thought. It certainly made sense that whenever Chase Winfield felt like kissing a woman, he just went ahead and kissed her. So what else was new?

He smiled vaguely. "I've found it to be a most effective remedy whenever a woman starts yelling at me."

Diana's eyes narrowed. Did he have to add insult to injury? "I already said forget it, didn't I? We don't need an in-depth analysis of your actions!"

"Such a sweet child!" he observed dryly. He pulled his hand away. "So, we have the Harvest Ball at five dollars a ticket, and then we have the wonderful raffle. How much is that?"

"One dollar a chance." She twisted her lips. "I'm sure you would love first prize, Chase Winfield. It's a turkey."

He pulled his wallet from the back pocket of his jeans and removed a twenty. "That's for my admission and whatever's left I'll take in raffle tickets."

Diana counted out a length of chances from her roll of tickets. "Here you go. Fifteen exciting opportunities to try your luck."

"Thank you." He took the tickets from her and tossed them down on a covered chair. For a moment neither of them said a word.

She cleared her throat at last. "Well, it's getting late."

Suddenly, Chase said very softly, "Who are you, Diana Mueller?"

She swallowed. "I beg your pardon?" The look on his face was the exact same look he had given her five years ago, staring up at her from where he had lain on the cool sand. There was no way he could possibly remember it all now, could he?

"There's something about you . . ." Chase took a step closer and seemed to search her eyes. "What is it about you that bewilders me?"

Had he guessed? Diana started to tremble. Did he already know? By some bizarre quirk of fate, had he managed to recognize her after all these years? Hastily, she changed the subject. "I'm bewildered about something, too. Why are you buying up all the lakefront property?"

Her question shattered the mood, all right. Chase Winfield's jaw tightened perceptibly. "I can't tell you that."

"Why not?"

He averted his eyes. "Because it's—personal."

"Oh, really? And here I thought it was business!"

"I don't care to discuss it any further." His tone turned brusque.

"You don't have to," Diana flung back. "I'm leaving!"

"Wait a minute." Chase seemed to relent slightly.

"Thank you very much for your support of the Harvest Ball," she recited mechanically, "We of the committee all look forward to your presence." Diana edged her way toward the front door.

"Diana, listen." He followed close behind her. "It's not that I intended to be rude. It's just that there are certain matters I absolutely refuse to discuss with anyone."

She shrugged. "Honestly, Mr. Winfield, you needn't explain your actions to me. After all, we're only neighbors."

"I suppose that's true," he agreed, and opened the door for her. It was now dusk, and Chase appeared to hesitate a moment. "Can you find your way all right? It's nearly dark."

"Are you kidding?" Diana replied lightly. "I grew up around here."

The lean, tanned face loomed above her. "But is it safe to be wandering out alone?"

Diana fastened the ticket envelope shut. "Let me tell you about the crime rate in Silverwood Lake. The high point for the sheriff came three years ago when he finally solved a rash of burglaries. He ended up arresting a raccoon for breaking and entering. Seemed the little fellow couldn't resist bacon or potato chips." She stepped out onto the portico.

Chase laughed bleakly. "I'm beginning to think this entire village is something out of a storybook."

She lowered her head "It is, Chase. I really hope we can keep it that way."

"So that's what it's all about. You're afraid someone like me will change it."

She sighed wearily. "I don't know. What else should I think?"

A firm hand cupped her chin. "I wish you could trust me, Diana."

She looked up and tried to translate the expression

on his face, but it was unreadable. "I really wish I could, Chase," she responded, and without waiting for his response bounded down the steps and across the overgrown lawn.

"Hey, Diana!" he called out after her. "Wait a minute!" Without thinking, Chase started to follow, but realized it was too late. She had already disappeared into the shadows. He stared out into the night with a perplexed expression on his face. He stood out on the porch for a long time, his gaunt features a mirror of the confusion in his mind. What had possibly possessed him this evening? How could he have permitted himself to lose control like that? He'd never intended to kiss Diana. Of course, he would be lying if he didn't admit that he had enjoyed that kiss immensely, but it was beside the point. She was only twenty-one, and he was thirty-five. She was far too young. And there was still the other matter, the business that had brought him up here in the first place. He hadn't told anyone, not even his lawyer or the other members of the board. It was hardly their affair, but when he'd suddenly announced his taking of a leave of absence, it had caused quite a stir within the company. Yet, he hadn't explained himself to anyone for over ten years, and it was certainly not necessary to begin now. This was his own business, not the company's. He owed explanations to no one. And soon it wouldn't even matter. Soon, if he had his way, the lake would all belong to him.

Chapter Five

Diana tossed and turned that night; she simply couldn't fall asleep. She was unable to stop thinking about what had transpired at Chase Winfield's house. He had kissed her so suddenly. Obviously, it had just been an impulse on his part. He probably made a career out of kissing any woman who came within ten feet of him. Besides, what was it he had said? *I've found it to be a most effective remedy . . . .* With an ego like that, who needed all the hot air in the Goodyear blimp?

Still, on her part at least, the kiss had been most disconcerting. In high school, and later in college, she had never reacted to a kiss in quite that way. Just because Chase Winfield was so attractive, so overwhelmingly masculine, that was not sufficient cause to allow a casual kiss to go to her head. Maybe when

Mavis Gumbler was a young girl a kiss meant something more. But the age of chivalry was long gone. Nowadays, most kisses were meaningless.

Diana sank her face into the soft feather pillow. What was the point? She sighed restlessly. She would never be able to sleep. The moonlight filtering in through the open curtains illuminated the alarm clock on the nightstand. It was only two o'clock. She pulled back the bedclothes and padded over to the window in her bare feet. Beyond the back lawn, the lake glimmered under the night sky, aglow with countless stars. The water seemed to beckon her. The effect was hypnotic.

For the first time in five years she answered the eerie summons. Silently, she pulled the cotton nightie over her head and fumbled in the dim light for her pale blue swimsuit. It dangled carelessly from a hook inside the closet door, a lightweight racing-style garment in the thinnest of nylon. Diana had purchased it at the college bookstore during her freshman year. It still bore the faded white emblem of the school in tiny letters across one hip.

Diana slipped it on quickly, and made her way downstairs. It was a balmy September night, with barely a breeze ruffling through her long, loose hair. Except for the sound of crickets, she was completely alone.

Once down by the water's edge she let her toes sink into the wet sand. It never occurred to her for an instant that anyone would possibly be watching. The hour was far too late, and there was not a single light on in any of the homes along the shore. Slowly, she made her way into the water. It lapped around her legs gently, caressing her. In one fluid motion she plunged forward, submerging her entire body for a brief moment. How delicious it felt! Diana turned over on her back and floated for a while. She had no concept of how much time had passed, and it didn't really matter anyhow. This was all hers; this was Diana's enchanted kingdom. In the veil of night her private paradise could never be taken from her.

Feeling relaxed and, at the same time, totally refreshed, Diana started to make her way back to the shore. The moonlight danced on the rivulets of water gleaming down her body. Her soaking brown hair hung long and dark across her shoulders and down her back. Slowly, she emerged from the lake. Only then did she see him.

Chase Winfield stood on the sand, perfectly still. He stared at Diana in absolute incredulity. The instant she became aware of his presence, she froze in her tracks.

Chase continued to stare at her in silence, as if he were seeing her for the first time. Neither of them moved. And then, after what seemed like an eternity, he finally spoke.

"It was you all along, wasn't it, mermaid? It was you that night!" His voice came out as barely a whisper.

Diana couldn't have run even if she had wanted to. There was no place to go. Chase took several steps toward her, successfully blocking her path. His stunned gray eyes combed every inch of her face and traveled hungrily down her body, pausing at her breasts, where the hard points of her nipples were clearly outlined beneath the wet, clinging bathing suit.

"It wasn't a dream after all, mermaid," Chase murmured. "It really did happen, didn't it?"

Diana shook her head to deny it, at once panic-stricken. "I—I don't have the faintest idea what you're talking about!"

Chase moved closer. "I should have put it all together before. Pete Turner, the old man who supposedly saved me—he's your next-door neighbor, and your good friend."

"Saved you from what?" Diana feigned ignorance.

"Oh, come now, mermaid." He smiled triumphantly. "There's no reason to deny it now. You're my sea nymph. You're the one who pulled me from the water that night."

This was a different Chase Winfield talking, and Diana was more frightened than ever before. At this moment he was not Chase Winfield the businessman. He wasn't even Chase Winfield the playboy. Right now he sounded more like the exhilarated romantic of five years ago. What made it even more frightening was that this time he was cold sober.

"Do you know why you can't deny it, little mermaid?" Chase read her thoughts once more. "I'm not seeing you through an alcohol-induced haze. You're no drunken hallucination now!" He reached out a hand. "You're real, and I can touch you." His fingers drew a line across her lips, down the pulse of her throat, and paused where her bathing suit plunged in a deep V between her breasts.

"Please!" she protested softly.

"Please what?" he whispered back.

"Don't touch me like that!" She tried to pull back, but by now his other arm had captured her waist.

His silver eyes glittered. "But, mermaid, I want to touch you like that, and like this!" Chase tipped back her head and buried his fingers in her gleaming wet hair. "What ever happened to those silver combs you wore that night?"

"Let me go!" she insisted weakly.

"Oh, no," he declared. "Not this time." His mouth hovered tauntingly above her neck, his warm breath fanning her cool, moist skin.

Against her own volition she was being drawn into his spell. "You don't understand!" Diana continued to protest, every muscle in her body defying her.

His eyes narrowed. "Do you want to know what I understand, mermaid? For the past five years you let me believe it had all been a dream—a wonderful, enchanted dream." Chase's voice grew hoarse. "Now the dream is over. This is reality!" He pulled her roughly to him and took her mouth with a harsh urgency. His kiss was a mixture of both anger and desperation. Chase punished her with his marauding mouth, forcing apart her lips and probing the sweetness inside with his hot tongue. Diana gave an involuntary shudder and yielded to his passionate assault. A moment ago her arms had hung limply at her sides; now they stole up around Chase's neck, stopping to learn the texture of his sleek black hair.

"Yes, that's it!" he approved in a low moan. His hands traveled past her waist to rest on her hips and fit them tightly against his hard thighs. His lips continued to punish, teach, and persuade. They left her mouth to caress her cheeks, her forehead, her eyelids. He planted endless kisses along her earlobe, down the tenderness of her throat, and, finally, he pulled aside one narrow strap and kissed the smoothness of her bare shoulder.

"Chase!" His name escaped her lips breathlessly.

"So soft, like velvet!" he murmured. "I always imagined your skin would be like this!" Chase's weight suddenly shifted and he drew her down with him onto the cool damp sand. His long, powerful body surged against hers, the fabric of his slacks rough on her bare thighs. His sure hands pulled the remaining strap of the bathing suit down to expose her other shoulder. He caressed it with practised fingers.

Diana lay lost in the wonder of his embrace, thrilling to the touch of his mouth as it once again plunged into the moistness of her own.

"How could I not have known?" he whispered over and over between kisses. "The moment I saw you I should have realized!" Again he teased her lips apart and drew the nectar from her as if her mouth were a honeyed flower. But then his hands began to pull the top of her swimsuit down farther to reveal her breasts. "So beautiful! Just as I knew you would be!" Chase's urgent fingers descended onto each silky mound.

The pleasure of his touch was exquisite, but a thousand warning bells started going off in Diana's mind. "Stop it!" she cried out.

Chase ignored her, lowering his hungry mouth to one nipple.

"Chase, please!" she pleaded, struggling beneath his onslaught. She could not allow him to continue touching her in such an intimate manner. Diana tried to wrench herself free from his powerful grasp.

Chase raised his head and stared down at her, his eyes dark with passion. "I want you," he breathed raggedly, a stark finality to his words.

"No!" she cried out softly as he imprisoned her resisting body between his legs.

"I want you *now*, my beautiful little mermaid!" Tenderly, he stroked the strands of smooth brown hair back from her forehead. This overtly innocent gesture caused Diana to panic even more because it was more subtly possessive than any other caress he had given her. In that split-second she knew that Chase Winfield had every intention of making love to her, right there on the beach.

"Don't do this, Chase!" She sobbed, and for the very first time, the fear in her words penetrated through to him.

"Diana?" he gazed down at her in astonishment.

"Don't do this!" she repeated, a strange poignancy to her plea.

Chase took a long, deep breath and attempted to check his desire. "Are you saying you don't want to?"

Diana nodded mutely, still trapped beneath his hard male strength. She turned her head away, unable to bear the intensity of his gaze.

Chase reached out a hand and cupped it under her chin, bringing it toward him. "I can feel you trembling beneath my fingers. You want it as much as I do."

She couldn't stop the trembling, and his probing eyes seemed to plunge straight into her soul.

There was an odd kind of urgency in his voice. "Answer me, Diana!" He lay there above her, waiting for an affirmative reply, but her silence continued.

Diana's hands moved instinctively to cover her naked breasts, gleaming white with the translucence of a pearl in the moonlight.

"Don't," Chase murmured in a raspy voice. "Don't hide your loveliness from me!" He stilled her hands. "I promise I won't touch you—yet. But please, just let me look at you!"

The raw emotion in his words shook Diana to the core of her being, but no man had ever seen her half-nude body before. "No!" she finally said in a tremulous whisper. "Don't look at me!"

"Have I made you shy, little mermaid!" Chase

inquired thickly, every word a taunting caress. "Are you blushing beneath that soft, sweet skin?" As he spoke he relinquished his tight hold on her. Diana seized the opportunity to roll away from under him. "What the—" He was caught completely by surprise. Chase reached out to pull her back to him, but wasn't quick enough. She sprang up from the sand with the agility of a young fawn and darted toward the woods.

Chase rose heavily to his feet and stumbled after her. But he had not grown up on Silverwood Lake. He did not know every tree, every bush, every pocket of thick underbrush the way Diana did.

"Wait!" he called out, his startled gray eyes scanning the landscape in frustration. "Where are you going?"

His prey was crouched low behind a massive boulder, her heart beating faster than it ever had before. As a child she had often played hide-and-seek behind this very rock, the sides and crevasses soft with moss. It never occurred to her, back in the blissful innocence of childhood, that she would be using this favorite hiding place years later, in a far more adult game.

Chase waited in vain for an answer, the muscle in his jaw growing tight as he stood somewhere amid the shadowy recesses of pine and rock. "Diana, answer me!"

She kept perfectly still as the man called out her name over and over again. His footsteps crackled across the blanket of crushed leaves, the crumpled

NO OBLIGATION . . . Each month we'll send you 6 brand-new Silhouette Romance novels. Your books will be sent to you as soon as they are published, without obligation. If not enchanted, simply return them within 15 days and owe nothing. Or keep them, and pay just $1.95 each (a total of $11.70). And there's never an additional charge for shipping and handling.

SPECIAL EXTRAS FOR HOME SUBSCRIBERS ONLY. . . When you take advantage of this offer and become a home subscriber, we'll also send you the Silhouette Books Newsletter FREE with each book shipment. Every informative issue features news about upcoming titles, interviews with your favorite authors, even their favorite recipes.

So send in the postage-paid card today, and take your fantasies further than they've ever been. The trip will do you good!

CLIP AND MAIL COUPON TODAY!

NO POSTAGE
NECESSARY
IF MAILED
IN THE
UNITED STATES

BUSINESS REPLY CARD
FIRST CLASS PERMIT NO. 194 CLIFTON, N.J.

Postage will be paid by addressee

Silhouette Books
120 Brighton Road
P.O. BOX 5084
Clifton, NJ 07015-9956

remains of a hundred autumns in nature's cycle at the lake.

"Diana, please!" His deep voice was now tinged with a layer of concern. "I want to talk to you!" His footsteps came closer. "Why are you running from me?"

There was a haunting familiarity to everything that was taking place under the eerie moonglow. In very much the same way Chase Winfield had first come upon her five years ago. Diana was cringing low behind a boulder, and the tall panther was stalking her just as he had one night in the past. He spoke in the same coaxing, beguiling tones that he had used on that fateful September night. But now, however, he was even more dangerous because he wasn't dizzy from the effects of too much liquor. This time he was wide awake and fully in control. This time he would not pass out on the sand. He would not reprieve her by falling into a peaceful, heavy slumber.

"Diana!" he called out again. "Where are you?"

She tried to slow the pace of her rapid breathing, and willed him to go away. Her heart was hammering as she dipped her head even lower against the protective rock. The footsteps stopped. *Please,* she prayed silently, *please go away. Give up and go home now, Chase Winfield!* It was true that he frightened her, but in a way she was more frightened of herself. How easily she had given herself up to his seductive charm. How effortlessly he had been able to persuade her with his hard hands and sensuous kisses. He had very nearly succeeded in seducing her tonight, the only thing that had saved Diana so far had been her initial fear of the unknown, her very inexperience. Chase must not be permitted to touch her again. She had no way of knowing how long she could hold out against his special brand of magnetism. He was so sophisticated and masterful, the combination was overpowering. If he made love to her, there would be no holding back. She knew he would take everything she offered and more.

Suddenly, behind her a twig snapped. "Listen to me, Diana." There was a long pause, and she realized that even though he was barely a few yards away, he still could not see her. "I'm in no mood to play any more games tonight!" There was another pause. "If you stay out here much longer, you'll catch cold." He hesitated. "Can you hear me?"

Diana didn't budge, didn't even move a muscle. The concern in his tone had turned to irritation. She didn't trust Chase Winfield. Not by a long shot.

He was more than merely annoyed now. "I'm a bit too old to be playing hide-and-seek. Aren't you?" He gave an inaudible curse. "Diana!" Chase had apparently reached the end of his patience. "You're a little tease, do you know that?"

Diana tightened her mouth, resisting an urge to shout back at him angrily. The nerve of that man. The gall of him! She hadn't been the one to tease him. Hadn't *he* just tried to seduce her? Hadn't *he* been the one who had initiated the lovemaking? Hadn't he been the one who had uttered words of rough passion and carried her down with him onto the sand? Could he deny that she had struggled? Diana blushed. Well, perhaps she hadn't struggled as much as she could have, but still, he had been the seducer. Chase Winfield was so used to having his way with women, it probably never even occurred to him that a woman might not want to make love with him on demand. He was so very sensitive, in fact, Diana thought bitterly, that he could not even detect her fear, her inexperience.

"Have it your own way, Diana!" Chase finally declared harshly. "I'm leaving now!" His footsteps receded into the woods. She waited ten minutes before raising her head. Then slowly, she made her way back to her own house and up the steps of her porch.

Locking the door behind her, she ran up the carpeted staircase to her bedroom. She rolled off the damp, sandencrusted bathing suit and tossed it into the bathtub. Grabbing a fleecy terry-cloth towel, she vigorously began rubbing all the dirt and sand from her arms, legs, and back. Even her breasts were coated with a thin layer of beach residue. She brushed her skin harder, as if attempting to remove more than just sand. She was trying to whisk away the memory of what had been experienced down on the shore with Chase. The friction only served to make her skin red and tender; the disturbing memory remained.

He had held her, and she had trembled in his arms, not merely in fear. He had touched her body with hands that were well-versed in how to give a woman pleasure, and seemed to draw her very soul from her lips. Diana could still feel the imprint of his mouth, searing its heat across her neck and between her breasts. She shuddered at the recollection of ecstasy half-fulfilled. She looked in the mirror as she touched her lips, bruised and still throbbing from his many kisses.

"Chase!" she whispered at her reflection. He had carried her down upon the sand with words hoarse with passion and need. He had called her beautiful, a word no other man had ever used to describe her. For a few moments at least she had known what it was like to feel beautiful. And desired.

Diana shut off the bathroom light and crawled into bed. Curling up between the soft, flowered cotton sheets, she attempted to shut her eyes tightly and clear her troubled mind.

"Why did you ever have to come here, Chase Winfield?" she murmured into her pillow. "What do you really want from us? From me?" She drifted off into a dreamless slumber.

Chapter Six

At six-thirty the next morning Diana was awakened by the loud buzz of a helicopter flying low overhead. She later found out from Frank Ramsey that the helicopter bore the logo of Winfield Enterprises.

"It was just about sun-up," he told a rapt lunch-hour crowd at the E-Z Break Snack Bar. "I'd just unloaded my power mower off the back of the truck—as you know, that Winfield fellow hired me to spruce up the grounds. Anyhow, this whirlybird comes out of nowhere, hovers over Grey Lodge for a few minutes, and then *whoosh!* It lands right there on the front lawn, and a couple of guys in suits climb out." Frank shook his head incredulously. "I'm telling you, my eyes just about popped out of their sockets. Anyhow, they start banging on the front door, and Winfield throws it open and starts yelling at them in words I never even heard in the navy." He laughed, running his fingers across his scraggly mustache. "Then these business-suit guys start pleading with him, and he keeps shaking his head. I'm telling you, that man looked mad enough to shoot a rabbit. And the next thing you know, he's gone back into the house and brings back this briefcase, and all of them climb into the helicopter, and they take off. I never saw anything like it."

Diana sealed the lid on her container of hot tea and placed it into the paper bag alongside her usual blueberry muffin. She handed the exact change to the counterman and waved good-bye to everyone. Once back in her car, she drove the short distance to the clinic. It was another busy morning, with Dr. Myers out on a call. Yet for obvious reasons, she was grateful for the heavy workload on this particular day. At least this way she wouldn't be thinking constantly about Chase Winfield. The fact that he had flown away early in the morning, and could very well be hundreds of miles away by now, made her feel a bit more comfortable.

Diana had just eaten her lunch when Pete Turner, who had never given Diana even the slightest indication of his plans, stopped by the clinic and mentioned to her that he had petitioned the town council for an emergency town meeting. The subject to be discussed was the rather sudden acquisition of lakefront property by Chase Winfield.

"It's high time the matter was discussed!" he exclaimed to Diana.

She peered at her friend curiously. "It didn't seem to bother you before."

Pete leaned over the counter and tossed a folded newspaper toward her. "Page seven."

Perplexed, Diana unfolded the paper and turned several pages over. "What am I supposed to be looking for?" It was a week-old business periodical published in New York City that Myra MacPhee stocked during the summer season for tourists beginning in June and running through October.

"You'll see it. An article about a big land deal that's in the works in some 'secluded village' in upstate New York." Pete's lips tightened. "Well, honey. Read it."

How could she possibly have missed the caption? It said "New Expansion for Winfield, Inc., Revealed." The story quoted reliable sources concerning secret plans for the building of a new site of operations. Chase Winfield, the chairman of the board and president of Winfield Enterprises, Inc., categorically denied any such plans for a multi-use industrial complex to be constructed in the village of Silverwood Lake. The article quoted Mr. Winfield as calling all rumors "unfounded" and "irresponsible." It went on to say, however, that the young industrialist admitted to having purchased substantial real estate holdings in the area. He refused to reveal the purpose behind these acquisitions. The news item ended with the disturbing quote:

> Once again, Winfield the Wunderkind has displayed his usual lightness of foot in beating all competitors in the frantic race for corporate growth. The Silverwood project, though still tightly under wraps, promises to set even more wheels spinning in the business world. What new scheme can C.W. possibly be cooking up this time?

"Well?" asked Pete. "Do you see now why I requested a special meeting?"

Diana shook her head sadly. "Oh, yes." In a way, she wasn't really surprised by any of this. On the other hand, she couldn't help being just a little disappointed. Perhaps, in the back of her mind she had been secretly hoping that the man had more honorable plans for the property he had been steadily acquiring. What was it that Chase had told her? That his reasons for wanted to buy up all that land were personal? Well, maybe to a dyed-in-the-wool businessman like Chase Winfield plans for corporate expansion were what he meant by the word *personal.* It was obvious that the two of them used different dictionaries. Why had she even doubted that the man was nothing but a ruthless manipulator of people? Why had she even questioned his motives? She should have at least learned something from her experience of the previous night. Chase Winfield was used to taking what he wanted, whenever he wanted it. Women or land, what did it matter?

"I wasn't really worried before, Di, and that's the truth!" Pete confessed. "I could have sworn that Winfield was a guy who wanted to get away from it all." He paused. "When he bought the Grey place and started buying up all the adjacent lots, I thought the worst that could probably happen was he'd build one of those millionaire-type hideaways for himself . . . maybe turn the lake into a golf course or something!"

Diana laughed bitterly. "So, instead we'll probably end up with smokestacks and chemical spills."

"Not if we can stop it."

Diana quirked her eyebrows. "But Pete, if he owns all the property, how can we stop him from doing whatever he pleases with it?"

"The council can still put a few impediments in Winfield's way if the members move fast enough."

Diana pursed her lips thoughtfully. "Are you thinking of any council member in particular?"

Her old friend grinned. "I'm thinking of the youngest and most recent member of the council. Her name, as I recall, is Diana Mueller." He thrust his plump hands back into the pockets of his baggy overalls and jangled the loose coins inside. "She's a little dynamo, that Diana. I hear she's becoming a very influential new voice in local politics.

Diana handed Pete back the newspaper. "Flattery will get you everywhere." She hesitated. "Do you think we can really stop him, Pete? He's an awfully big cat and we're just tiny little mice."

Pete sighed. "Well, we can sure as heck give it one good try!"

The meeting was set to convene at eight o'clock the following evening. Chase Winfield was still out of town. According to a cable news station, he was supposedly engaged in labor negotiations at one of his California plants. Diana was almost relieved he wouldn't be around when the special town meeting was held. After all, it was open to every resident who wished to attend. Anyone could speak up and be heard. That was democracy in action.

That night it seemed the entire village was there. Everyone had an opinion on the subject. Frank Ramsey stood up and exclaimed angrily that he didn't want Silverwood turning into an "industrial nightmare." Others were concerned about all that property in the hands of one owner. What would it do to their fishing rights? Henrik Schuyler wanted to know. There were others who declared vehemently that they had a legitimate right to sell their own property and nobody was going to stop them. At that point tempers flared and pandemonium broke loose.

Willy Sutherland, the senior council member, had to bang his gavel a half-dozen times before order was restored. Diana, sitting up front with the other council members, shifted uncomfortably in her seat. She had never seen this many people so riled up before. After all, it was a sleepy little village, and life usually went on in a pretty relaxed fashion. But it was beginning to look as if Silverwood Lake was now splitting into two very distinct factions. She didn't like it one bit, and it was all Chase Winfield's fault. Why couldn't he have picked on some other town?

When it came his turn to speak, Pete Turner reminded the people in the audience, most of whom he had known their entire lives, that the lake was one of the few untouched natural wonders left in the state. It was practically pollution-free. "It isn't something a single person can own. It has been left in trust for us, and for future generations," he pleaded. Well respected in the village, Pete could have held any office he wished but simply wasn't interested in local politics.

When the council adjourned the meeting it was announced that the entire matter would be taken under advisement. Diana was placed in charge of a committee to research the situation.

"And what does *that* mean?" She flung her hands up in the air.

Willy Sutherland folded his gold-rimmed spectacles back into the pocket of his threadbare velvet jacket. "Well, Diana, it will be up to you to check the stacks of old records in the clerk's office and discover if there are any obscure zoning ordinances or local covenants that could specifically preclude development of the lakefront."

"Could you repeat that in English, please?"

He smiled patiently. "My dear, at this point it appears there are no laws presently on the books to prevent Mr. Winfield from doing whatever he pleases with his property. Current zoning restrictions do not apply to lake property."

"Are you saying that if there are any ancient statutes, decaying in some dusty file drawer—"

"Then it's up to you to find them!" He patted her on the shoulder.

"But Willy," she protested, "I'm no lawyer!"

"All you need is patience, good eyesight, and a group of volunteers to help you. If you're fortunate enough to find something, start worrying about *his* lawyer!" Willy lit a match and kindled his tobacco. Nothing ever seemed to perturb the antiques dealer. Sometimes Diana wondered if Willy had strong emotions about anything. Just as this thought was going through her mind the senior council member raised an eyebrow. "Of course, if Chase Winfield is going to continue to buy up every lot in sight, there's always one thing you can do."

She looked up hopefully. "What's that, Willy?"

"Not sell!" He gave a high-pitched laugh and took a long, thoughtful puff on his pipe.

The following afternoon Diana and several volunteers on her committee spent a total of four hours poring over the old records in the clerk's office. They didn't find papers that could apply to the situation, although at one point Sara Lee Hutchins lifted her freckled face from a sheaf of musty documents and grinned. "Hey, Diana! Did you know it used to be against the law to own more than one goldfish?"

"Cute, Sara. Real cute." She nearly tossed an old magazine at her.

"Oh, let me see that!" cried out Helga Schuyler. "It's from 1955. Look who's on the cover." She grabbed the magazine. "Marilyn Monroe!" Helga started flipping through the pages excitedly.

"Boy, they never throw anything out in this room!" declared Sara Lee, pulling out another box. "Would you believe this old carton is filled with programs from the 1933 all-county high school production of Gilbert and Sullivan's *Mikado?"*

"Do you guys mind?" Diana blew a layer of dust off her white uniform and reached for another box. "This is starting to sound like a pajama party! We've got a lot of work to do."

The two other women exchanged glances. Helga sighed. "Oh, Diana, you're always so serious."

"But this *is* serious!" she protested.

"Helga's right," said Sara Lee. "You should really lighten up a little." She leaned over toward Diana. "We volunteered, didn't we? If we find something, we find something. If we don't, well, such is life."

"That's a wonderful attitude," Diana observed wryly. "Don't you want to save the lake?"

"Of course we do, but that's no reason to stop smiling, is it?" Sara Lee struck a pensive pose. "To be absolutely truthful, there are far more serious issues at stake besides the welfare of Silverwood Lake."

"Name one."

"Oh, I'll name the most serious, urgent crisis

facing us today—why can't the three of us meet any guys?"

Diana couldn't help laughing. "There's always Miles at the gas station. I've seen the way he looks at you, Sara Lee."

"Bite your tongue!" She paused. "So, tell us about Chase Winfield. I hear he came into the clinic the other day. Is he as gorgeous as his picture?"

"Is he coming to the Harvest Ball?" chimed in Helga.

Diana rolled her eyes in complete exasperation. They'd never get any more work done at this rate. She could predict that her so-called committee would soon consist of one active member: Diana Mueller. It was high school all over again.

By the time Diana finally arrived home, stumbling through her front door with a small sack of groceries, it was nearly seven-thirty.

"I've been waiting for you," a cool voice announced several feet away from her.

"What the—" She almost staggered into a nearby lamp as her eyes caught sight of a steady trail of cigarette smoke rising up from the high-backed easy chair facing the other direction.

"What is it with the people in this town?" continued the familiar cynical voice. "Doesn't anyone lock their doors? Total strangers could just walk right in."

Diana strode around to the front of the chair and stared at the intruder. He wore an immaculate three-piece gray suit, which matched the glint in his eyes. His long legs were stretched out carelessly on the coffee table, and a cigarette dangled from his mouth.

"What are you doing here?" she finally asked.

"I already said what I was doing here. Waiting for you!" He took a final, deliberate drag from the cigarette and stubbed it out in the small crystal ashtray.

"How dare you just come into a person's house when she's not there?" Diana demanded.

Chase swung his lanky legs off the table and rose to his feet. "Is that any way to greet a person you haven't seen in three days?" Without waiting for a reply he reached out, pulled the paper bag out of her arms, and carried it into the kitchen.

"Now, just a minute!" She marched after him angrily.

He set the bag down on the counter.

"Chase Winfield, what are you doing in my house?" She thrust her hands onto her hips.

He folded his arms across his chest and stared at her for a long moment. "Are you genuinely mad at me, Diana, or is it simply an act?"

She tried counting to ten to control her building rage. "Mad, Chase Winfield? Let me tell you something. You haven't *seen* mad yet." She resisted an urge to ruffle his perfectly styled black hair with a nearby eggbeater.

"Give me your best shot," he replied. "I'm sure I can handle it."

Diana walked slowly toward the formica counter.

Pointedly ignoring the towering interloper, she began emptying the contents of the shopping bag. She could feel Chase's eyes burning into her.

"Go ahead." There was a subtle taunt to his words. "I'm still waiting."

She set a box of spaghetti down with a loud smack. "What do you want from me, Mr. Winfield?"

"Oh, so now it's 'Mr. Winfield!' "

She attempted to shrug with appropriate nonchalance. "Why should it be anything else? I'm on a first-name basis only with *friends.*"

His eyes narrowed. "After the other night I would surely think that 'friends' would more than adequately describe you and me, Diana."

"I don't want to talk about the other night!" She threw open a wooden cabinet door and tossed a box of spaghetti inside. "And you're no friend of mine, Mr. Winfield!" Diana slammed the door shut again.

"But *I* want to talk about it." Chase looked at her sharply. "Why did you run away from me?"

"I told you, I don't care to discuss it." Diana tightened her fists into balls, keeping them clenched at her sides. Why couldn't he leave her alone? She couldn't stand the tumult of emotions his presence was causing.

"We're going to discuss it," he insisted, striding over to her swiftly. "Because I'm not leaving here until we do."

In business Chase Winfield made a formidable adversary. In love he was far more difficult to contend with. And as he stood so close to her in the small kitchen, Diana realized with horror that despite everything, she was falling in love with him. Or perhaps she had been in love with him since the first time she had seen him five years ago. Good heavens! How ludicrous to discover you are in love with somebody during the middle of an argument. "This is ridiculous!" she declared aloud.

"I agree," Chase responded, misunderstanding her completely. "I held a vibrant, passionate woman in my arms that night, and suddenly she turned cold on me. I want to know why."

She averted her eyes. "You started it. I didn't ask you to."

His hand descended on her wrist. "Oh, you certainly asked, little Diana. Every time you looked at me with those huge amber eyes of yours."

She vainly attempted to twist her arm free. "Of all the conceited, arrogant—"

"Why did you go swimming in the moonlight?"

"That's none of your business!"

"You knew I would see you." Chase smiled confidently.

"At two o'clock in the morning? You've got to be kidding!" She was incredulous.

"You wanted me to see you like that, in the water."

"You're crazy!"

"Am I?" He tightened his grasp. "That's what you wanted me to think all these years. That first time I saw you, I was sure I was going crazy. Later, I never quite believed Pete Turner's story about finding me on the beach. I still couldn't explain you, though. You were real, yet you weren't real." Chase pulled her toward the fine wool of his vest. "Why did you hide from me back then, anyway?"

Diana glared. "You have to *ask?*"

"You saved my life that night! I wanted to thank you."

"That wasn't all you wanted to do."

He looked away uneasily. "So you just let me think you were some kind of illusion . . . that you never really existed."

"For heaven's sake, I was sixteen years old!"

"You're not sixteen now," he replied in a husky tone. "Why didn't you let me finish what we started?"

"For the last time, *you* started it, not me," she retorted hotly. A flush spread upward across her face at the remembrance of his delicious lovemaking. Why did he have to stand so close? She could feel his breath above her forehead and smell the musky tang of his after-shave lotion.

"You're blushing again," he murmured wonderingly. "Do I really have the power to make you do that, little mermaid?"

She instinctively raised a hand to cover the bright pink tint on her cheek. Betrayed by her own body. How mortifying!

With surprising gentleness he peeled the fingers away from her petal-smooth skin. "It's too late to hide it now, so why even try?" One hand kept her wrist still tightly pressed against his chest while the other traveled across her face to linger maddeningly on the sensitive lobe of her ear.

"Don't!" She quivered involuntarily.

"Your mouth is always crying 'don't,' but the rest of you shouts shouts 'yes!' " A finger teased its way along the delicate column of her throat. "Feel how you vibrate to my touch."

Being next to him was like reacting to a powerful drug. Diana felt herself being pulled in toward his sensuous web. "Egomaniac!" she accused him breathlessly. "Arrogant beast!"

Chase's silvery eyes narrowed. "Keep hissing like an angry little kitten. You know how it excites me!"

"Macho pig!" she added furiously.

"Flattery will get you everywhere," he whispered. "For starters, come *here!*" He forced her chin upward and took her lips with his own. The split second of contact was electric. The nerve of the man!

He raised his head several inches above hers. "I've never tasted anything like your mouth. It was made just for me!" He returned to her lips, savoring all her textures, his hands pressed against her slim back.

I must fight him, Diana thought desperately. *I won't let him control me like this.* She yielded but did not respond. She stood limply within the circle of his arms, allowing him to take her, but refusing to follow.

The intensity of his kisses increased as Chase tried to cajole, persuade, and finally force a response. His hard mouth grew bolder, prying her lips apart to induce a more intimate caress. With every inch of her will she attempted to remain impassive.

At last Chase drew back, bewildered. "Diana?"

With deliberate casualness she glanced up. "Are you quite finished?"

He stared down at her with an odd harshness. "You don't mean that!" He pulled her back against him angrily and kissed her with a violence she had never known before. He bruised her tender lips and blazed a trail of fiery caresses down her throat. Diana's heart was hammering beneath her rib cage, but she maintained an iron control and continued to lie against him, apparently unmoved.

Again Chase drew away. "What's happened?" he grumbled.

Diana forced an indifferent shrug. "If you're quite through playing the caveman, I have to start cooking my dinner."

The air was still, and Chase shook his head in disbelief. "I don't understand any of this! The other night—"

"What about the other night?" She gave another shrug. "Honestly, the ego of some men!"

"For goodness' sake, Diana! Tell me you don't mean it!" His jaw tensed.

His tone of self-doubt was so unexpected that Diana stared up at him in astonishment. "Chase?"

"Please!" he begged in a hoarse whisper.

Seeing a self-assured man so suddenly humbled

made her heart fall to the bottom of her stomach. Could this possibly be Chase Winfield the sophisticated playboy? Was this actually the same arrogant man who only moments before had stood there confidently, secure in his supreme male attractiveness?

"For the love of heaven, say something!" He shut his eyes for a long moment and gave a pained sigh. "Do something! Anything! Just give me some kind of response!"

Diana couldn't believe her eyes. Was he actually trembling? Unconsciously, she brought a hand to his cheek. She could feel a muscle throbbing beneath her fingers.

"Yes," Chase breathed, "touch me!" He stood perfectly still.

With unpractised hands she pressed his head toward hers, her slender fingers raking hesitantly through his thick ebony hair. Chase's hard mouth hovered scant inches away.

"Don't stop," he pleaded. "Whatever you do, don't stop now!"

Slowly, Diana pulled his head down the rest of the way, until their lips barely touched. She had never been the aggressor before, and it felt both awkward and tantalizing. She planted a light, butterfly kiss on each corner of his mouth. Still not sure of herself, Diana's mouth journeyed gently along his jawline.

"Yes!" he approved huskily. "Do anything you want."

With a dizzying sense of freedom she returned her lips to his mouth and brushed it tentatively.

"Explore me," he growled. "I won't bite, honey."

Diana's petal-soft lips pressed against his closed mouth. "Like this?" she murmured.

"Yes!" A strange tremor colored his voice. "Go on, please."

"Chase!" she whispered shyly. "I don't know how!"

"You're doing just fine, love."

Diana swallowed convulsively and wrapped her arms even tighter around his neck. This movement unconsciously thrust her breasts against his warm chest. "Like this?"

"God, yes!" Chase's entire body immediately went tense.

Diana's lips lingered briefly on his rough cheek. It was so erotic to savor him at her own pace, to taste his salty flavor with increasing confidence.

His hands drew tiny circles upon her back in a soothing rhythm. "Sweet little Diana," he murmured. "Come closer to me!" The hands traveled lower, until they found her hips, and clasped her against him possessively. She could feel the frank evidence of his arousal between his muscular thighs. It was shocking, yet for some strange reason she could not pull away. Instead, she relaxed against him—immobile, transfixed.

"I went too fast the other night," he confessed. "I was an idiot. Only a fool would rush you!" His eyes glittered down into hers. "I want to take my time with you. Hours and hours, mermaid." With a low groan he drew her mouth back to his in a new kind of kiss. It was teasingly slow, a molten heat melting any last thought of resistance from her. Diana's lips parted in astonishment and answered the searching need of Chase's questing mouth. His tongue probed her own inner core and the shock waves reverberated through her entire body.

"Oh!" The exquisite sensations he was awakening inside her were startling.

"I want to kiss the breath out of you!" he muttered thickly.

Diana shivered in the glow of his desire. Never in her life had she felt so beautiful, so wanted. Every romantic fantasy she had ever dreamed was coming true at this very instant. The real world, if there was one, evaporated completely from her thoughts. The only reality was right here, with Chase making slow, deliberate love to her. She buried her head against his smooth cotton shirt just above the V of his vest. He wore no undershirt, and she imagined she could hear his heart beating beneath the thin material.

"Feel what you do to me?" he murmured against her silky hair.

How glad she was that she did wait until this very moment. It was worth everything, even the loneliness, to have saved herself for this man. Chase nibbled a hungry trail along her earlobe, and she moaned with pleasure.

"Do you like when I do that, honey?" he whispered. "I want to taste every inch of you tonight." The nibbling continued past her earlobe, down toward the base of her throat. A deft hand unfastened the top two buttons of her white dress and exposed more creamy skin to his gaze. His eager mouth seared its way toward the shadowy cleft between her breasts. "Do you want me to kiss you there?" Chase muttered hoarsely.

Diana nodded mutely as shudder after shudder racked through her. Was it wrong to feel this way? Was it wanton to thrust herself so intimately against a man's body? Or to want him to keep touching her in thrilling new ways?

All at once Chase gave an inaudible cry and scooped her up in his arms. Without a word he carried her out of the living room and up the unlit staircase. Diana's heart pounded rapidly as she felt him pause at the top of the landing and fumble for the light switch.

"Show me your bedroom," he whispered huskily.

Diana flushed a deep crimson and silently pointed down one end of the hallway. In several long strides he had reached the tiny room, hesitating in the doorway before approaching the narrow bed, with its frilly pink canopy. He stood there, clutching her tightly in his arms, and stared at the bed. Then slowly, he lowered her to her feet. "My God," he exclaimed. "You're just a child!"

She looked up at him in puzzlement. "Chase?"

He raked a hand through his disheveled hair. "I must have been out of my mind not to have figured it out. No wonder I frightened the hell out of you the other night!"

"Chase?" she repeated, unsure of the strange look that suddenly came into his eyes.

"You're a virgin, aren't you?" he asked raggedly.

Diana bit her lip in embarrassment. "Does it matter?"

"It sure as hell matters!" His voice was harsh.

"But Chase, I—" She was about to tell him that it was all right, it didn't matter about her being a virgin. Nothing mattered, because she was in love with him.

"Do you think I could touch you now?"

She took a step toward him questioningly. "I don't understand? What have I done?"

"That's the problem," he replied bitterly. "You haven't done anything!" He stalked over to the doorway, shaking his head in disbelief. "Twenty-one years old, and you haven't done a blasted thing yet!"

Diana's eyes widened. He was actually angry at her! There was a long, painful silence. "Does this mean you don't want me anymore?" she asked in a small voice.

He exhaled sharply. "What do you think I am? Some kind of monster?" He clenched his fist. "You should have told me before!"

She threw up her hands in frustration. "You never gave me the chance!"

"That makes it even worse," he rebuked with suppressed rage. "Do you realize what very nearly happened?"

"But Chase," she protested. "That shouldn't make any difference if—"

His eyes narrowed. "If what?"

"If two people—" Diana stopped herself. She had been about to say *if two people love each other,* but she suddenly realized the enormity of such a confession. *She* loved him, of that she was now sure. But Diana was struck with alarming clarity that she had no concept at all of Chase's true feelings for her. And it was a strong possibility that his feelings, if any, might not run very deep. She was naive when it came to men, but it was a distinct possibility that while Chase Winfield could be passionate, and even romantic, that he might not be capable of love. He had made it very clear how how much he desired her. She was an object to be pursued and won. After he finally caught her, well, that was a different matter. A playboy didn't suddenly change his stripes overnight.

"If two people *what?*" Chase probed darkly.

She turned her head away in embarrassment. "Nothing." How could she even hint at her feelings now? Wasn't it obvious from his cold reaction that he no longer wanted to have anything to do with her? A man who truly cared for her would be delighted to discover that she was still a virgin. He would be pleased that no other man had ever touched her in an intimate way. A man who truly cared would be infinitely tender and patient while he proceeded to teach her the many pleasures of love. "Nothing at all," she repeated in an anguished tone.

He read the pain in her eyes. "Oh, God! Don't make it any worse than it already is!" Abruptly, he left the room.

Diana heard his footsteps thudding heavily down the staircase, and, a moment later, the loud slam of the door. Unbidden, the tears started to well up in her eyes.

"Chase!" she whispered. "Why couldn't you have loved me back?"

Chapter Seven

Much to Diana's relief, she saw very little of Chase during the next two weeks. She seldom ventured along the beach anymore, and apparently, he, too, avoided her like the plague. Not once did she hear the hum of his motorboat. On the rare occasions that they ran into each other in the village, their conversations were stilted and awkward. One morning, at the post office window of Myra MacPhee's general store, Diana was busily engaged in an animated conversation with several of the regulars when Chase strode in to pick up his mail.

"And how are you this fine morning, Mr. Winfield?" inquired Myra solicitiously. She wanted to know so she could be ready to regale the community with any new gossip.

Chase smiled vaguely at the middle-aged woman.

"Yes, the weather is very pleasant Miss MacPhee." He wasn't about to give Myra new grist for her mill, but the woman never lost hope.

"I declare, Mr. Winfield, no one in Silverwood Lake has ever gotten the amount of mail that you have!" She hoisted a large envelope through the opening in the window. Chase accepted it politely and turned to walk out the door. It was then he noticed Diana for the first time.

"Hello, Diana." He gave her a curt nod.

"Hello," she replied uncomfortably. She didn't care that the entire store was watching their exchange with great interest. The only thing going through her mind at that moment was how incredible the entire situation was. Nothing in her past experience had ever prepared her for a man who could burn hot and then suddenly turn cold. And the chill was most certainly in the air. Chase Winfield, who had trembled with passion in her arms not so long ago, now stood before her, frosty and remote.

"How is everything going at the clinic?" he inquired briefly, his expression unreadable.

Diana averted her eyes. "Just fine." she said dully.

Chase stood there, hesitating for a moment, as if he were debating whether or not to say something else. But he quickly changed his mind and turned away, heading toward the exit. Diana prayed that no one else would see her pain. Why did she have the misfortune to have fallen in love with a man who couldn't love her in return? How long would it take for this affliction to run its course and for her to get over him? If it were a real disease, at least she could consult Dr. Myers. But it was love, a malaise she was quite unfamiliar with until now. Probably, the only cure was time. Well, she certainly had plenty of time, for all the good it did her.

"So, little Di." Her thoughts were interrupted by the voice of Willy Sutherland. "How's the committee coming?"

Diana looked up at the thin little antiques dealer. "We still haven't found anything yet."

Willy played idly with his pipe. "Well, dear, don't be discouraged. Keep looking."

"Of course," she replied, still somewhat distracted. Right now she was beginning to wonder if she cared about saving the lake anymore. During the past two weeks she had begun to feel confined and claustrophobic. Perhaps there really wasn't much of a future for her in this quiet little village. Maybe Anna Smith was right about there not being much to stay around for. Since the shattering incident with Chase, the enchanted spell the lake had always woven about her seemed to have dissipated.

It came as quite a surprise that very afternoon when Chase Winfield phoned her at the clinic. "I was wondering if you were free for dinner this evening," he asked in an odd voice.

Her stomach tightened into a ball, and she exhaled nervously. "Why?"

His irritation was revealed loud and clear through

the receiver. "A simple yes or no will suffice, Diana."

That made up her mind for her. "I'm sorry," she snapped. "But I'm busy."

"Do you have a date?" he asked sharply.

"I don't see where it's any of your business!" Her hand was still shaking when she slammed down the receiver. How dare he presume to question her? What right did he have to pry into her private affairs after he had made it very clear that he wanted nothing further to do with her? Diana was forced to admit that his sudden interest had gladdened her aching heart. On the other hand, she instinctively knew that it would be wrong to give in to Chase Winfield. He could break her heart too easily.

A minute later the phone rang again. "Don't you ever hang up on me again!" boomed the angry voice on the other end.

It was about time someone taught that man a lesson, Diana thought with a bitter smile as she slammed the receiver down once more. She might be lovestruck, but the only creature permitted to bark at her was Hans. Then the phone rang a third time.

"Before you hang up again," Chase informed her tersely, "this is a business call."

"Oh?" she replied. "Are you ill?"

"Of course I'm not ill!"

"You said it was a business call, Mr. Winfield, and this is a clinic. One would naturally assume you might be sick." She made sure her tone was as sweet as could be.

Diana could hear a long sigh on the other end of the line. "Are you still there, Mr. Winfield?"

"Yes," came the chilly answer. "I mean business as it concerns my property."

"What do you mean?" Her heart fell.

"I want to arrange a time for the two of us to get together and discuss the actions of your committee." There was a brief pause. "When would it be convenient for you to meet with me?" His voice was stiff and extremely formal.

"I really don't—"

"Of course, tonight is out of the question," he sneered. "As you've made it quite clear that you already have other plans."

Good heavens, he actually sounded jealous! But that had to be her imagination playing tricks on her. As far as Diana having "other plans" was concerned, well, since when did she ever have a date in this secluded town? She had a date all right, with a TV dinner, but she certainly wasn't going to let Chase Winfield know that. Why should she give him the satisfaction? Besides, it was too late to take back her lie now.

"Are you still there?" Chase asked.

"Yes."

"Well, then. Is tomorrow evening all right with you? Or are you otherwise engaged on that night, too?" he asked sarcastically.

Did he have to be so insufferable? She took a deep breath. "Tomorrow is fine."

"Very good. Shall we say about eight o'clock?"

Much to her amazement, the pencil she was holding between her fingers suddenly snapped in two. "Eight o'clock it is. Where do you want to meet?"

There was a brittle silence. "I'll come and get you."

"That's hardly necessary!" Diana exclaimed.

"I said, I'll come get you at eight o'clock!" Chase retorted in a voice that brooked no refusals.

After this rather baffling invitation Diana was unable to concentrate for the rest of the day. So, what else was new? She shrugged at the mirror in the clinic's rest room as she refreshed her face with a wet paper towel. Ever since Chase Winfield had returned to Silverwood Lake she had been unable to think straight. There was a definite advantage to her previous state of mind. Before, when her heart had been unawakened, life had been so simple and uncomplicated. She might have been lonely, but at least her world had been safe and soothing. There had been no wild forays into the murky, uncharted waters of alien passions.

After work she spent longer than usual at the clerk's office, combing relentlessly through more dusty boxes. Helga and Sara Lee dropped by ostensibly to help out. Both women were now teachers at the central high school, and their workday ended at about the same time Diana's did. She was happy for their company but suspected that the true purpose of the visit was not committee work, but rather to socialize.

"Why don't you give up trying to find any obscure record?" remarked Sara Lee as she leafed through another ancient magazine. "If you really want to see something interesting, take a look at this photo spread on the new starlets of 1951. I've never seen so many blondes with black eyebrows!"

Diana ignored her, pausing beside another sealed carton. "I wonder what's in here."

Helga yawned. "So, Diana. What are you wearing to the Harvest Ball this year?"

"A dress," replied Diana distractedly, probing the outside markings of the carton for some clue as to its contents.

"Helga," Sara Lee interrupted, "are you going to wear your Miss New York State Pageant gown again this year?"

The statuesque blonde groaned. "I'll be wearing that blue chiffon monstrosity for the rest of my life."

Diana looked up thoughtfully. "But it's a lovely dress, Helga. You always look so beautiful in it."

"It's nice of you to say that, Diana. Frankly, I'm getting a little tired of wearing the same thing year after year. But what choice do I have? My mother never lets me forget how much money she shelled out for it during the contest." She sighed. "Anyhow, tell me about your dress."

"It belonged to a great-aunt of mine," Diana said. "I've never worn it before."

"One of those frilly things with a high neck?" inquired Sara Lee.

Diana shook her head. "Actually, it's from the

1920s. I understand my mom's aunt was a regular flapper."

"Sounds fabulous," Helga remarked enviously. "I wonder if Chase Winfield is going to show up at the dance."

Diana was absorbed in ripping open the top flap of the cardboard carton. "I think we might have something here!" Meticulously, she began leafing through the papers inside.

"Do you think he knows how to polka?" Sara Lee wondered aloud. "Diana? What do you think?"

But Diana wasn't listening to the idle chatter. She was staring, transfixed, at a yellowed document. "I don't believe it."

Helga crouched down beside her. "What did you find, Di?"

She turned to smile at her friend. "I think we've found what we've been looking for." Diana scanned the aging scrap of paper once again, just to make sure. "Yes!" She shouted triumphantly. "We've done it!"

"I don't get it," said Sara Lee. "What did you find in that old box?"

Diana gave each of them a hug. "This single slip of paper is going to save our lake!"

"But what is it?"

"You're a social studies teacher, Sara. Do you know what a restrictive covenant is?"

"You're kidding! You mean there actually is one, after all?"

Diana sighed in relief. "Oh, yes. Indeed there is."

Her smile broadened. "And I'll bet a few people are going to be exceedingly surprised." One, in particular, she added to herself.

She couldn't wait to see the expression on Chase Winfield's smug, arrogant face when he found out about the existence of this precious document. Diana had never been a vindictive person; it would have gone against her gentle nature. But Chase had hurt her very deeply, and a part of her cried out for satisfaction. She wanted to be the bearer of bad tidings, to witness the look on his darkly handsome face when he learned that money couldn't always buy him everything. This would be one time, at least, that he couldn't get what he wanted.

"Do me a favor, gang," she said to both women. "Don't say anything about this until about eight o'clock tomorrow night."

Helga looked at her curiously. "Why?"

"Because we've known each other since nursery school, and I'd appreciate if you could keep this a secret for just a little while."

Sara Lee shrugged. "We can keep a secret, can't we, Helga?"

The older woman smiled knowingly at Diana. "So, you want to tell him yourself, huh?"

Diana blushed bright crimson. That Helga Schuyler was a double threat. Beautiful *and* smart. No wonder she wasn't married yet. For the first time Diana wondered how Chase would react to someone like Helga. Surprisingly, a pang of unbearable jealousy streaked through her.

"Hey, is anybody hungry?" She quickly changed the subject. It was agreed that they should all adjourn to the Village Tavern for hamburgers and beer. The three of them had not eaten dinner out together since high school, and it proved to be a rather pleasant diversion. Diana had forgotten how enjoyable a "girls" night out could be. She lost all track of the time, and it was midnight when she pulled the car into her driveway.

It was in considerably high spirits that she went upstairs to bed, the precious piece of parchment under lock and key in the clerk's office. "Just you wait till you find out about this, Chase Winfield," she whispered out loud to the wallpaper. "And Helga is right. *I'm* going to be the one to tell you!"

Chapter Eight

Diana dressed for her Friday evening meeting with great care. While she knew very well this was not a date, she still wanted to look her best. It did wonders for a person's self-confidence, after all. There was a great deal of pride involved, too. Diana wouldn't have been completely honest with herself if she didn't admit that she wanted Chase to see her dressed attractively for a change. After pulling out half the contents of her closet, she finally settled on a favorite red cotton knit dress. It had contrasting blue piping on the neck and sleeves and a matching navy leather belt, which accentuated her slim waist. The simple, understated dress was from her college days, yet the soft material still clung flatteringly to her young curves. She decided to leave her hair loose, falling in gentle waves past her shoulders.

Chase rang the doorbell promptly at eight o'clock, his expression dark and foreboding. Tonight he was in a deep chocolate-brown jacket of the supplest leather, and a pair of perfectly fitting corduroy slacks. It was yet another expensive outfit that only Chase Winfield could wear with that indefinable air of casual luxury. He took several reluctant steps inside the hallway, silently taking in all the details of Diana's appearance.

It made her nervous, the way he continued to just stand there, without saying a word. "And a good evening to you, too!" she finally remarked sarcastically.

Slowly, Chase took a long, deliberate breath. "Where were you last night?"

It was the last thing she expected him to say. "I beg your pardon?" Maybe she hadn't heard him correctly.

His eyes narrowed into hard gray slits. "I asked you where you were last night."

"And since when is that any of your business?" she retorted.

His mouth tightened ominously. "Answer my question, Diana."

She gave an indifferent shrug. "I don't see where it's any of your business."

"Your car wasn't in the driveway when I came by last night." He glared at her. "It was well after eleven."

Diana's heart began to hammer in her ears. "And what, may I ask, were you doing here at that hour?"

"That's not the point!" he insisted.

"Oh? How interesting." She reached for her sweater. "What is the point?"

He stilled her arm. "We're not going anyplace until you tell me what you did last night!"

She jerked her arm away. "I already told you it's none of your business!"

"It is my business," Chase hurled back tautly.

Conflicting emotions thundered through Diana's confused brain. "Read my lips," she announced shakily. "I don't owe you any explanations, Chase Winfield. I don't need to account to you for my actions." She gathered the delicate angora cardigan around her shoulders. "Can we go now, please?"

Chase didn't move. "Whom were you out with, Diana?"

Angrily, she turned to him. "Why don't we forget the whole thing? If you really want to have a meeting with me, let's just have it right here and get it over with!"

"Who was he?" His tone was harsh.

"How dare you!" she said in a choked whisper. "How dare you presume to expect any explanations from me?"

"It's the least you owe me," he snarled.

This time Diana didn't bother counting to ten before she exploded. "I owe you nothing, do you hear me? Nothing!"

"Did you let him touch you?" The words were like razor blades.

Diana's lips parted in surprise. "What?"

"Did you let him make love to you?" His voice was sharp.

"What do you take me for?" she raged in disbelief.

He gave her the blackest look she had ever seen. "You just couldn't wait, could you? You had to go straight into another man's arms."

Was that what he really thought? As if she could even permit another man to touch her after knowing the exquisite pleasure of Chase's kisses. And for him to stand there now, pointing an accusing finger at her! It was just too much to bear. "Of all the nerve!" Diana's blood boiled. She was shaking all over, unable to stop herself from lashing back at him in hurt and frustration. "How could you?" The tears began to well in her eyes. "It's not enough that you come here and tear my life apart. It's not enough that you tell me how much you want me and then drop me like a hot potato." She averted her eyes painfully. "But now you burst in here like a madman, demanding to know my whereabouts, and accusing me of being little more than a tramp!"

There was a long silence. When Diana finally looked up, the blood had drained from his face and he was as white as a sheet.

"God!" he groaned. "What have I done to you, mermaid?" He took a step closer and gazed down into her tear-filled eyes. "I never meant to cause you any pain." With gentle fingers he cupped her chin toward him. "I never intended to hurt you." A salty drop rolled down Diana's cheek. With unexpected tenderness Chase wiped away the glistening tear. He gave a tortured plea. "Don't cry, love, I couldn't bear it if I made you cry."

"What do you care?" she said dully.

He shook his head. "Oh, I care." There was an odd sadness in his voice. "Believe me, little Diana, I care."

She sighed. "I don't know what to believe anymore."

Chase dropped his hand back to his side. "Do you think I could have lived with myself afterward, knowing I'd taken a virgin?"

She gave a defiant shrug. "You're assuming a great deal. "The fact is, I never exactly came out and said I was a virgin."

He burned her with a scalding glare. "What are you saying?"

"Did you ever hear me actually admit that I . . . that I never . . ."

He grasped her wrist savagely. "You little idiot! Can't you see that I can just look at you and know the truth!"

She struggled ineffectually in his angry grip. "You wouldn't know the truth if you tripped over it!"

"That's exactly what happened, I tripped over it. Be thankful that I did, Diana. A few minutes more and it would have been too late. Nothing would have stopped me." The muscle in his jaw tensed. "Do you know what that would have done to me? How I much I'd have hated myself—but worst of all, how much *you'd* have hated me for taking your innocence."

Against her own volition Diana glanced up into his pained silver eyes. "No," she whispered. "I could never hate you."

His hand brushed her forehead. "Yes. You would have hated me, mermaid. I wouldn't have known enough to be gentle the first time. I'd have hurt you, all right." He rebuked himself. "I wouldn't have held anything back. Not with you." He released her and turned away quickly.

"Am I supposed to thank you?" she uttered painfully.

"You're not supposed to do anything," Chase ground out. "It doesn't matter anymore."

Diana looked at him questioningly. "Why?"

His voice was distant, strained. "Because the situation is not going to come up again, that's why."

The stark finality of his words made her wince. "I see," she said quietly.

"But there's no reason why we can't still be friends," he continued. "You'd like that, wouldn't you?"

Diana nodded mechanically. "Of course." Friends! How could she bear it? Being so close and yet not being able to touch, not having him hold her and kiss her.

He cleared his throat. "It's for the best, Diana."

She forced a brittle smile. "I know."

Uneasily, he turned away to glance at his gold

wristwatch. "And there's no reason why we also can't maintain a business relationship. That's what I wanted to discuss with you this evening."

It's over, she told herself painfully. *It's over, even though there's so much we could have given each other.* How could he just turn himself off like that? How could he possibly believe that it was truly for the best? Was he so wise and she just incredibly naive? The sad part was, Chase actually believed that what he was doing was the right thing. In an odd way, he was acting chivalrously.

Fine, just fine, then! If he could do without her, she could very well do without him. She could behave with just as much maturity. She could forget that he had ever whispered words of passion against her lips. She could forget the maddening tide of desire that had swept over them both. She heard herself say in a controlled, calm voice. "Certainly, Chase. I see no reason why we can't behave like adults."

He smiled briefly, but the smile did not reach his eyes. "I'm glad you feel that way, Diana. It makes this all so much easier." He strode over to the front door and held it open for her. "We really have to reach some sort of understanding concerning the town council, and your committee."

Ah, business! It always came down to business, after all. Diana followed him out the door and into the night air. His blue Mercedes gleamed in the reflection of the porch light.

They drove silently down the lake road, Diana too

engrossed in her own thoughts to initiate a conversation. After several moments of silence Chase turned to her and remarked, "I thought we'd find a quiet place to have dinner and talk."

"Whatever you want." She shrugged indifferently. She was somewhat surprised that Chase intended to take her out to dinner. For some reason she had assumed he just wanted to talk briefly about the committee and leave it at that.

Chase glanced at her sharply, but didn't say anything further. It was a forty-minute drive to the small inn at the town of Fralinglitch, the county seat. Although the setting was rustic, the ambience was quite elegant. A white-gloved maître d' escorted them to a table set with linen and crystal.

Diana felt somewhat underdressed for a Friday night. Chase looked at her curiously. "Are you uncomfortable?"

She glanced around the room at the well-dressed diners. "It's just that I didn't know we'd be going anywhere quite so fancy."

To her amazement Chase suddenly reached across the table and put his hand over hers. "If you're really ill-at-ease, we can go somewhere else, but the food here is supposed to be terrific." He smiled soothingly. "Look at how I'm dressed. Did you see the glare that waiter gave me when we first came in? But I've spent my entire life not giving a damn what other people think. That's what got me where I am today. Besides"—he paused—"this setting becomes you, Diana." His hand tightened, and she quivered involuntarily. Quickly, he released her from his grip and turned to the menu.

"What would you like to have?"

Diana really wasn't very hungry. The contretemps in the living room had taken away her appetite. She shifted in her seat uneasily. "Actually, I eat my big meal in the middle of the day."

Chase continued to scan the huge gold-colored menu. "Would you like me to order for you?" Obviously, it was something the man did all the time. He fit into the restaurant with such incredible ease that the difference between being an ordinary person and a wealthy, powerful man, used to giving commands, became suddenly evident to Diana.

She barely tasted the shrimp cocktail or the chateaubriand for two that Chase had ordered. She went through the motions of eating the superbly prepared cuisine, but the food just didn't have any flavor. This was a new kind of emptiness, a different type of loneliness. Even though Chase was an excellent dinner companion and was extremely polite throughout the meal, the strain between the two of them was obvious. Diana was hardly aware that her wineglass had been refilled several times. She was far too nervous to be conscious of anything other than the fact that the man she loved was sitting just a short distance across the table, and the only thing he was interested in was whether or not the town council was in a position to place any obstacles in the way of his plans to acquire more property.

"I had no idea that you were a member of the

council," he remarked, lighting a cigarette. "Isn't it unusual for someone your age?"

Diana took another sip of the burgundy. She seldom drank, but for some reason tonight was different. The delicious beverage relaxed her considerably. "There was a special election last May, after the council representative from my district passed away."

Chase took a long drag. "So, they elected you."

There was another uncomfortable pause. "I might as well let you know now, Chase." She leaned forward, resting her chin between both hands. "The council will never approve your development plans."

He peered at her in confusion. "What development plans?"

"It's no secret. We know all about the industrial complex you intend to build here."

The cigarette nearly dropped from his mouth. "Industrial complex . . . on the lake? Are you out of your mind?"

"No. But you are if you think you can get away with it." Diana couldn't understand why Chase looked so shocked. Did he actually think that they were such rubes that they weren't aware of his plans?

He shook his head in disbelief. "What gives you the idea that I'd even consider using Silverwood for an industrial development?"

"We know, Chase. It was all over the New York papers."

His eyes narrowed. "And do you believe everything you read?" Viciously, he stubbed out his cigarette. "Just because it's printed in a newspaper, that makes it the truth?"

Diana gestured helplessly. "What are we supposed to believe? You come to our town and start buying up every parcel of land you can get your hands on. You're willing to pay well over the market value . . ."

Chase looked down at the table. "And so you automatically assume I'd do something as insensitive and short-sighted as destroying your lakefront." He let out a deep sigh. "That's what you think of me?"

Diana was baffled at his reaction. "What else would motivate a businessman?"

"It never occurred to you," he countered in a low voice, "that I might have other plans for the property.

"What kind of plans?"

A shadow covered his expression. "It doesn't matter what they are. The point is you are always willing to assume the worst."

"Presented with the nature of the evidence, our assumptions were extremely logical." It was Diana's turn to look doubtful. "Are you going to sit here and tell me that everything we've read in the papers is untrue?"

"Yes."

He actually expected her to believe that. Whom was he kidding?

"Of all the places in the world where I might possibly choose to expand my operations, Diana, why would I do it here?"

She shrugged. "Who said it had to make any sense?"

He glanced at her coldly. "Your faith in me is overwhelming."

"The *last* thing I should have in you, Chase Winfield, is faith. Don't even bring that word up in my presence." Her caustic reply surprised even Diana.

"What are we talking about now?" he asked suddenly. "I thought our discussion concerned the council and your committee."

"It does."

"Are you sure? Or are we really discussing something completely different?" Chase's gray eyes glittered across the table at her. "Are we actually talking at cross-purposes?"

He could still do it! The way that man was able to read her mind was frightening, she mused. Fortunately, the wine had numbed her reflexes slightly. The alcohol somehow managed to erect a protective wall between her mind and her heart. How long it would last, she had no way of knowing. "Mr. Winfield—" she began slowly.

"Chase," he corrected her.

"Mr. Chase," she started again, oblivious to his amused smile. "Do you know what a restrictive conevent . . . I mean a covenant—" Heavens, she was tipsy! She'd never been drunk in her entire life. Across the table she could see Chase grinning from ear to ear. He thought it was the funniest thing in the world.

"Do go on," he urged her politely, his lips twitching.

Diana was furious. He had done it; all of it was his fault. He'd sat there all during dinner, pouring more and more wine into her glass, and now she couldn't even speak straight. How absolutely mortifying!

"You were saying something about a restrictive covenant?" Chase queried, struggling to keep from laughing out loud.

So he thought the entire thing was a joke, did he? With every last vestige of control Diana made a concerted effort to draw herself up straight. "We found an old document just last night," she said, speaking slowly and clearly. "It was drawn up by the original owner of the property over a hundred years ago. With the exception of the two children's camps that were set aside specifically for that purpose, the land was deeded to a succession of owners with the proviso that it only be used for private residences." She smiled smugly at her flawless delivery.

Chase leaned forward. "Is that all?"

"What do you mean, is that all?" Diana nodded confidently. "Let me assure you, that while the document is old, I've been informed by several lawyers that it most certainly is valid."

Chase shrugged carelessly. "I'm delighted to hear it."

"How can you be delighted?" she asked. "It means you can't use the property now."

He sighed. "If I ever told you my real reason for wanting that property, you would never believe me." He reached across the table once more and placed a firm, warm hand over hers. "Diana, Diana. I don't intend to do anything that would violate any covenants or the natural beauty of your wonderful lake. And you can tell *that* to the members of your town council."

She stared at him wide-eyed. "Are you serious?"

"Dead serious," he responded. "If I'd had any idea how anxious everyone was, I certainly would have cleared up this little misunderstanding sooner."

"But I don't understand—"

He silenced her by placing a finger on her lips. "You don't have to understand, Diana. All that's necessary is that you believe me."

"But—" she protested. "what reason would—"

"I told you before," he interrupted. "My reasons are personal ones. Too personal to discuss with anyone." He looked away. "Perhaps one day I'll tell you about them. But not now."

The drive home was a quiet one, the only noise coming from the excellent speaker system in the Mercedes. Chase had put on a stereo cassette recording of Debussy. The soothing orchestral strains filtered through the car as Diana leaned back drowsily against the comfortable leather seat. Chase didn't talk much along the way. He kept his eyes straight ahead on the road, occasionally glancing in her direction. The next thing Diana knew, they were in her own driveway and Chase was gently nudging her on the shoulder.

"Sleepyhead," he murmured. "We're home. Time to get up!"

"Hmm?" she said groggily, sinking deeper into the buttery-soft seat.

"It must be the wine that's putting you to sleep," he declared, opening his own door and coming around to the passenger side. He leaned over and unfastened her shoulder harness. "Are you very comfortable?"

"Uh-hmm." She was floating now on a fat, fluffy cloud.

"I see where I'm going to have to give you a hand," Chase decided. Before she could protest he had scooped her into his arms and lifted her from the car. He carried her across the gravel to the front door.

It felt so good, so warm, to be enveloped by his strength. He was all supple leather and musky skin against her body. She was only half conscious, and from far away she heard a deep, amused voice.

"Naturally, you didn't bother to lock your door."

"That's nice." She breathed drowsily, feeling some reply was expected of her even if it didn't make any sense.

She could feel herself being carried up the carpeted staircase. With every step she seemed to bounce gently against his warm, hard chest. Diana gave a satisfied murmur and snuggled deeper into the cradle of Chase's arms.

"You're purring like a kitten," he whispered silkily. They were on the upstairs landing, and he was carrying her into her bedroom. In another moment he had gently deposited her on the bed, and was leaning over to slip her shoes off.

"Thank you." She heard herself sigh faintly.

"You're welcome."

Diana yawned and shut her eyelids as she began to drift off into oblivion.

"Diana." The clear, deep voice of Chase Winfield reached her somewhere between sleep and consciousness.

"Uhmm."

The mattress tilted slightly as Chase sat down beside her. "Diana," he repeated gently. "Can you hear me?"

She gave a contented nod. "Umm. You sound nice."

"Thank you."

"But then," she continued with the lack of inhibition that only the combination of wine and extreme lethargy can produce, "you always sound nice."

"Do I?" came the soft response.

"Mmm. And you always look nice."

"Is that a fact?" The voice came very close to her ear, and suddenly she felt the brush of lips across her forehead.

"And you always kiss nice," she whispered.

"Oh, little mermaid." He breathed along her flushed skin. "You say the sweetest things!"

"Does that mean you still like me?" she murmured.

"Like you? *Like* you?" His voice was hoarse. "Oh, honey—it's beyond like." The bed sank deeper as it took more of his weight, as he leaned over and gathered her into the circle of his arms. "My lovely little Diana!"

"Oh!" she cried out sleepily. "Say that again."

He lowered his lips against her hair. "My lovely little Diana! So soft, so adorable!"

Was he really saying these endearments to her now, or was it all part of some wonderful dream? "Chase. . . ." She called out his name just to see if he was really there.

"Just one," he was whispering. "Let me have just one kiss to take home with me tonight!" His mouth descended onto hers, kissing her with exquisite tenderness.

Diana gave a small moan and opened her lips to receive his kiss more fully.

"Mermaid!" he uttered in surprise, and pressed her back against the mattress, slipping his hands beneath her hips so that her body arched upward into his. She felt his manhood surge against her softness, but there was nothing embarrassing about it. It felt so wonderful, so right. She wrapped her arms around his neck, and he groaned in approval, moving against her rhythmically. He freed one hand to move upward along her back to reach the zipper of her dress. In one fluid motion he had pulled it all the way down, slipping both sleeves off her shoulders and down along her arms. He buried his face in the softness of her bare skin, kissing her collarbone, her throat, her shoulders. Then his lips descended upon the valley between her breasts. Diana gave a convulsive shudder as he drew away the lacy pink bra to expose two perfect mounds.

"So beautiful!" he breathed huskily, taking one in each hand. He caressed and teased the peaks to hardness until Diana cried out from the divine pleasure of it. Then he took one rosy tip into his mouth and tasted its sweetness.

"Chase!" she moaned softly. "What are you doing?"

"Hush, darling," he whispered raggedly. "I won't let anything happen!" His tongue continued to flick her nipple back and forth, causing a tingling sensation to build deep inside her. She had never felt this way before. She had never wanted to get closer. Diana wasn't quite sure what part of her body the throbbing came from, but it seemed to radiate out in all directions. She pressed his short thick hair against her breasts, wanting an intimacy that was new and mysterious, yet as old and instinctive as time.

With a tortured exclamation Chase suddenly lifted his head. "What the hell am I doing?" In one swift motion he rolled away from her and off the bed.

"Chase?" she whispered.

"Good night, Diana." His voice was strained. "Go to sleep and forget this ever happened!" He stalked out of her bedroom and into the shadows of the hallway. Vaguely, Diana thought she could hear his footsteps pounding down the stairs. A few moments later there was the angry noise of a car engine, but by that time she had already drifted off to sleep.

Chapter Nine

When Diana looked back, the events of the previous night were all jelled into one hazy dream. She even wondered if it had actually happened at all. She sighed and tried not to think about it, but the memory of his hungry kisses kept coming back to her all day long.

Saturday was a particularly hectic day. It was the day of the single most important event of the entire year—the Harvest Ball. This year, like all years, Pete would come by and escort her in his pickup truck. There was no one else to take her, and frankly, even if there were, Diana couldn't think of anyone she'd rather have as an escort. Besides, it was nice not to have to worry about driving home alone. She felt slightly nervous, because although she was looking forward to the ball, Diana hadn't been to one in over two years. When her mother had died suddenly, she found it far too painful to attend the festivities they had enjoyed so much together. She could remember the three of them, piled into the cab of Pete's truck, singing old songs all the way to the recreation hall. It had taken all this time to dim the ache of such sweet memories and to start to enjoy the Harvest Ball again.

For the first time in two weeks she wandered down to the lakeside. Had Chase told her the truth last night, that he had never had any intention of developing the shore property into some kind of super-industrial monstrosity? He had never lied to her before, but still . . . No. She wanted to believe him. Even when he had pushed her away from his embrace he had always been honest with her. He had never promised her anything; he had never held out any false hopes in front of her. But even with Diana's relative lack of experience, she knew that something existed between the two of them. Something special and rare. Whether or not he chose to seek it out and nurture it to completion, Diana knew that it existed. He could deny it all he wanted, but somehow he always came back for more.

She wished her mother were still alive to give her advice. What guidance would she have offered her about Chase Winfield? What did a woman do when she fell in love but the feelings weren't mutual? How long did one wait? Did one wait at all? Or was love an instantaneous, mutual occurrence? She pondered this question, stretched out languidly on the sand in her white duck shorts and T-shirt. The midafternoon rays of the sun were still warm in this Indian summer.

Suddenly, the tranquility of the scene was shattered by the roar of an outboard motor. She propped herself up on her arms and saw the sleek silhouette of Chase's power craft skimming along the water. Her heart leapt at the sight of him, in sunglasses and a Rugby shirt, his black hair ruffling in the breeze. But at that exact moment she noticed the other passenger. She was blond and tall, dressed in the skimpiest of black bikinis. Even from this distance Diana could see that she had the kind of beauty that made Helga Schuyler pale in comparison. The young woman resembled an advertisement in a woman's slick magazine, the kind that shouted the message "if you use this fabulous perfume, you, too, can be as alluring as this glamorous model!" The woman gave a high-pitched laugh that was audible even over the loud hum of the engine. She saw Chase turn to her and nod. Then the woman leaned over Chase and whispered something into his ear, wrapping a possessive arm about him.

It was as if a sheet of glass had exploded outward from Diana's heart, shattering into bits. It was an explosion that hurtled debris of disillusionment and pain in its wake. So this was what it all meant. This was the true anguish of love. Never in her entire life had Diana known a moment of comparable misery. How could he? Just how could he? Only last night he had caressed her with such exquisite tenderness, and had barely been able to contain his need for her. And now, less than twenty-four hours later, he was basking in the warmth of a new flame. Was this what he had tried to spare her in the first place? Could this be the reason that he had been so reluctant to take her, knowing she was a virgin? Was it because he knew very well that he could not commit to anything more than a few nights of passion?

The roar of the motor became louder, and Diana thanked the heavens that her view was partially obscured by a clump of bushes. Perhaps he couldn't see her. She prayed the bushes hid her from his limited line of sight. There was something humiliating about his being able to see her like this when he had another woman in tow. The roar of the motor receded, and, mercifully, the boat disappeared from view.

Diana buried her face in her hands and began to cry softly. She couldn't stop the tears from forming, and she couldn't check the convulsive sobs that racked her body. She was completely overwhelmed by a dark disappointment. Now she had to face reality. She was not special to Chase Winfield. She was not something rare. She was merely another diversion, one of many for the millionaire playboy. How could she have ever doubted it? After all, she chastised herself, what ever made her think she was anything special? Was she still just clinging to that long-ago dream? The one where a mermaid had come from out of the night to rescue a drowning prince. It had all been a distortion. She had seen only what she had wanted to see. Now her eyes were open at last. Chase Winfield didn't want any involvements beyond sex. He didn't *want* love.

Diana stumbled through the rest of the day like one of the walking wounded. A strange numbness touched her from head to toe.

At six o'clock she took a long, luxurious bath and started to prepare for the ball. She tried to rid her mind of the image of Chase and the unidentified blonde, but nothing seemed to work.

"No!" she shouted aloud. "I won't let it ruin my evening!" She thought about Sara Lee and Helga, and how they, too, tried to have a good time, despite their loneliness. She thought about all the people in Silverwood Lake whom she loved, and how wonderful it was going to be to see them gathered together for one big celebration tonight. A warm glow crept into her heart, partially pushing away the cold chill. Pete. Willy. Mavis. Myra. Manny. How many hundreds of others could she name? Yes, it was going to be a lovely evening. She wouldn't allow anything to ruin it for her.

Diana resolved to look her best that evening. She would wear mascara and a bit of blusher, and do everything possible to make a lovely appearance. Someone had once said "Looking good is the best revenge!" Maybe that was right.

Linette Mueller had never worn the beaded gown left to her by her aunt Celeste. A true free spirit, Celeste had run away to seek the bright lights of New York at a time when such behavior on the part of country girls was viewed by their families as rather reprehensible. She had been a teenager during the late twenties, when Prohibition was still the rule of the day. Her destiny had been to become involved with a rather powerful bootlegger in Brooklyn. She later married him, never to return home again.

This dress was part of the contents of a trunk left in Celeste's Brooklyn home and later sent to Linette Mueller. But since Celeste had died only five years ago, a scant three years before Linette, the dress had never been worn by anyone else. In the first place, it was too small for Diana's mother to even consider wearing, and in the second place, it was far too sophisticated for Diana. But now, for her first Harvest Ball in two years, the gown was perfect.

It was the most elegant garment she had ever seen, a masterpiece of silk, bugle beads, and sequins. Like most dresses of the late twenties, it revealed, above its silvery fringe, a long expanse of leg. It ended high above the knee, and was cut above the breasts along the bias. The back dipped low, exposing an enticing amount of bare skin. Diana stared at her reflection in wonderment. This was an entirely different person looking back at her in the mirror. She shimmered and sparkled in a thousand different hues of blue and silver. It was hard to believe that a dress that was over fifty years old could still look so vibrant and fresh. She swept her hair up into a French twist and secured a silvery bandeau around her head. A tiny cluster of rhinestones in the center of the band sparkled and winked.

She strapped her feet into the delicate high-heeled silver sandals that had once belonged to her mother. At least they had been the same shoe size.

She critically surveyed the way her breasts were clearly outlined under the exquisite crêpe de chine. "Oh, well." She shrugged. "Let's go for authenticity, Diana!" She had never worn anything so blatantly sexy in her entire life. The truth was, she had never worn anything *remotely* sexy, either. "Well, good!" she declared. "It's about time you were the talk of the town, Miss Goody Two-Shoes!"

Pete, dressed in a straw hat and blue serge, took one look at her and burst into laughter.

"What's so funny?" she asked adamantly.

"You're a knockout, honey. An absolute knockout."

"So why are you laughing?" she said accusingly.

Pete graciously helped her into the pickup. "Honey, I'm laughing because I can't wait to see how many people you're going to knock flat on their ears tonight!"

The county recreation hall where the Harvest Ball had been held for the past fifty years had been built to replace the dance hall that had burnt to the ground in the Great Depression. The current structure was the focal point of all community events, but it was the Harvest Ball that really brought out its special beauty. Even though it resembled a huge barn more than a dance hall, with hundreds of balloons and streamers festooning the rafters the effect was always quite delightful. And this year the decoration committee, headed by Myra MacPhee, had truly outdone itself. The huge room was lit by hundreds of hanging lanterns in various hues, casting an enchanted glow over the cavernous hall. Naturally, amid the other decorations there were huge jack-o'-lanterns and dangling bunches of Indian corn.

Hundreds of people already thronged the huge dance area. At the moment the orchestra was playing "Apple Blossom Time," but the evening was still young. There were three different bands here tonight, playing everything from waltzes to cha-chas to polkas. Every generation in the county was represented, and the music belonged to everyone.

Pete had been quite correct in his assumption that Diana's attire would cause a sensation. Everywhere she went lifelong acquaintances turned to stare. It wasn't because her outfit was any more daring than many of the costumes being worn in the room, but it was because she, Diana Mueller, was wearing it. People just had never thought of her as anything other than demure, and maybe just a bit too prim for her own good. Besides, wasn't Diana Mueller the girl who wouldn't get dressed up if her life depended on it?

All around the room heads turned.

"Diana Mueller?"

"Hey, is that you, Diana?"

"Did you get a load of little Di?"

"You want to see something? Take a look at *that!*"

"Some dress, huh! See who's wearing it?"

So it went on all evening. Most people were genuinely pleased to see her looking so attractive.

"Diana," declared Miles, transfixed. "I didn't know you had legs!"

"Miles!" Sara Lee shot back, a vision in purple satin. "I didn't know you had brains!" She nudged Helga with a giggle as they watched the gangly filling station attendant whirl Diana onto the dance floor in a quick polka step. Diana danced every dance that evening. She waltzed with Pete, and did a fox trot with Frank Ramsey. She did the jitterbug with an amazingly spry Uncle Manny.

It was well into the evening, as she sat along the side with Helga and Sara Lee, when she noticed a familiar figure enter the hall. Her stomach knotted as she saw many of the locals greet Chase Winfield.

"Hey," Helga whispered. "Is that him?"

"Oh, what a hunk!" Sara Lee exclaimed. "I'm in love!"

Diana had to admit that Chase had never looked so devastatingly handsome. He wore a black tuxedo, which was, of course, superbly cut. He was easily one of the tallest men in the entire room. But even without his height he would stand out in any crowd. She saw the startled expression on his face when he noticed her, looked away, then stared at her again in recognition. She could tell her appearance surprised him.

"Oh, he's coming this way!" Sara Lee squealed.

Diana sat perfectly rigid, not wanting to speak with him, but also a little pleased that he looked so disconcerted.

"Diana."

At the sound of his voice she slowly raised her head. Chase was staring at her with a mixture of disbelief and admiration. "You look beautiful," he said softly.

"Thank you," she replied, slightly unnerved by the heat of his gaze. He was staring, actually staring. He drank her in from head to toe, caressing every inch of her with silvery eyes. The blood started pounding in her head again, and then she remembered that other woman, the blonde from the afternoon. She wondered why Chase hadn't brought her to the dance.

"Where did you get that dress?" he was asking, his gray gaze not leaving Diana for an instant.

"It belonged to her great-aunt Celeste," interrupted Sara Lee, giving Diana a sharp nudge with her elbow. "Introduce us, or I'll die!" she murmured under her breath.

"Oh, forgive my rudeness," Diana remarked with a faint smile. "Allow me to introduce my friends Sara Lee Hutchins and Helga Schuyler."

Chase extended his hand formally to each of the women, twisting his lips in amusement when Helga didn't let go immediately.

"I hope you don't think I'm being forward, Mr. Winfield," she said coquettishly. "But would you care to dance? They're playing my favorite song."

Chase shot Diana a helpless look and gallantly escorted Helga onto the dance floor.

"Boy," Sara Lee declared. "You've really got to hand it to Helga. She certainly knows all the right moves."

Diana folded her arms and watched the two of them dancing the quick steps of the bossa nova. Strange, but for some reason she knew there was no cause for jealousy. True, she still cared for Chase, and he had betrayed her with that as yet unknown blonde in the boat. Nonetheless, seeing him with Helga, she instinctively knew that Chase was not particularly attracted to her. Odd, because not only was the girl beautiful, she was charming. Yet the chemistry necessary for combustion was simply not there between the two of them. But then, she remembered that nothing existed between herself and Chase, either. Not anymore. But when would the pain go away?

The music ended, and Chase brought a flushed Helga back to them. He looked down at Diana again and said in a low voice, "We have to talk." But just at that moment there was a loud drum roll and a series of trills on the trumpet.

Out of nowhere Willy Sutherland appeared, quite dapper in formal dress suit with tails. "It's time for the dance contest, Di!" he exclaimed. With a perfunctory nod at Chase he grabbed Diana's arm and led her onto the dance floor. The reason Willy enjoyed dancing with Diana was that she was considered one of the outstanding ballroom dancers in the county. Ever since childhood her parents had told her how essential it was for a young lady to develop dancing as a necessary social skill. Her mother and father had won quite a number of contests in their day, and Diana, despite her shyness in other areas, continued to carry on the tradition. Willy Sutherland was now well into his sixties, but he carried himself with a grace seldom seen in men one-third his age.

"Let's do a tango," he whispered confidently. "It's our best number!"

Diana nodded as they waited for their turn on the floor. They were fifth in line to perform. And from the loud round of applause when she and Willy began their dance, it was evident that the crowd already knew who the winners would be. As Willy swirled her around and dipped her to the beguiling strains of the tango, Diana could see the tall figure of Chase Winfield watching wordlessly from the side. There was a surprised expression on his face, as if he had been taken completely off guard. Diana followed Willy's steps flawlessly, for over the years this particular dance and rhythm had become almost second nature to her. She imagined that Chase never expected she could dance so well. It was quite a delightful sensation to be at the center of attention in a hushed ballroom, wearing a delicious wisp of a frock that glimmered and sparkled underneath a single spotlight.

When the music ended, and Willy finished by dropping her nearly all the way down to the floor in one final deep dip, the applause was thunderous.

She and Willy took a bow, and when they left the dance floor, it was with the first-prize trophy.

"You keep it." She smiled at her partner, who flushed with pleasure. Amazing, how the littlest things could bring happiness to some people, Diana mused.

The orchestra started to play a slow dance and hundreds of couples began flooding onto the dance floor.

"I believe this is our dance," said a familiar voice behind her. Before she could object Chase had slid one arm around her waist and led her silently into the center of the room. Pulling her close against him, he led her easily along the floor.

"Have I told you how beautiful you are tonight?"

She could only nod, unable to come back with a snappy retort.

His silver gaze probed her face. "That was the sexiest tango I've ever seen."

Was that a compliment? Was she supposed to say thank you? Diana merely blushed and lowered her eyes to the satin lapel of his tuxedo.

"Blushing again?" he whispered huskily. "I've never known anyone so delightfully shy, Diana." His hand moved up along her back and touched bare skin. Goose bumps instantly formed beneath his fingertips. "Did I do that?" he breathed.

"It's the air-conditioning," Diana said quickly.

Chase buried his head in her hair. "There's no air-conditioning, you sweet little liar!" He brought her protesting body more intimately in touch with his. She could feel the hard lines of his muscular thighs and the beat of his heart through the thin silk of his dress shirt. He smelled of that wonderful, musky scent that was Chase. She relaxed against him at last. She simply couldn't help herself. It was the way he looked, the way he spoke, the way he felt . . . his distinctly male aroma. He was, to put it in the most basic terms, a feast for the senses. For a few moments she allowed herself the luxury of forgetting that other woman.

"Are you wearing anything underneath that dress besides naked skin?" he whispered into her ear.

"Chase!" she responded in a shocked whisper.

"Have I embarrassed you?"

"Yes!"

His breath was warm against her earlobe. "You shouldn't be embarrassed, honey. Everything about your body is exquisite!"

Mercifully, the music ended, and Diana was able to pull away from his grasp. He began to follow her off the dance floor, but was buttonholed by Myra MacPhee, who informed him most urgently that if he did not dance the next number with her, the consequences could be earth-shattering.

"I'll take all your mail and forward it to China!" she threatened with a wide grin.

Diana was frankly relieved to have escaped his net for a while. She sat off to a corner and watched the throng on the floor. She noted with a degree of pleasure that Sara Lee was finally dancing with Miles. He was holding her extremely close and the girl didn't seem to be raising much of an objection. Helga was wrapped dreamily in the arms of a tall, blond young man in an army uniform. Well, maybe for her two friends, love would finally find a way. Wouldn't *that* be something? She wished them both well, and then her eyes caught the tall, imposing figure of Chase Winfield and his partner, Myra MacPhee. She was throwing her head back and laughing hysterically at something he had just said. He certainly had her eating out of his hand. But then, why should that be so surprising? Women of all ages found him irresistible. Diana took a sip of apple cider. How long would it take for her to build up an immunity to his charm?

"Would you like to take a spin?" a vaguely familiar voice intruded on her thoughts. She looked up into the smiling blue eyes of Ricky Schuyler, Helga's older brother. As a young child she had always liked him, but as they had grown older, and he had gone off to college in the Midwest, she had forgotten about him completely. He was a brawny, muscular young man, with a headful of curly blond hair.

She smiled up at him. "Sure!"

"You really look fantastic tonight, Di," he exclaimed as they whirled around the dance floor to a disco beat.

How strange, thought Diana. Ricky Schuyler had been the most popular boy in high school. He had been captain of the football team and voted most likely to succeed. He was a male version of his sister

Helga. Handsome, likeable, and smart. Yet Diana felt no tingle of excitement as he held her close to him.

"Why didn't I ever ask you out?" he murmured against her ear.

Diana smiled in amusement. "Maybe because you weren't very interested, Ricky."

He groaned. "You mean I was stupid!" He paused. "What are you doing Saturday night?"

She rolled her eyes. "Where were you when I needed you, Ricky?"

"Seriously, Diana. Would you like to see a movie or something next Saturday?"

She shrugged. "I honestly don't know." He was a nice enough boy, but the truth was, Diana was reluctant to start anything with someone else. Had she been fifteen years old at this very moment, Diana would have been in ecstasy. Now, however, as she danced with her teenage idol, not a single bell went off inside her. Across the room Chase had finished dancing with Myra MacPhee and stood watching Ricky with a murderous expression on his face. Diana had come to know the significance of that tightening in his jaw, and a contrary imp inside her was secretly pleased at his discomfiture. It would serve him right if he actually were a little jealous. After what he put her through this afternoon! How she detested that hypocrite. He thought he could have his cake and eat it, too!

"Ladies and gentlemen, may I have your attention, please!" The shrill voice of Mavis Gumbler crackled over the microphone. The band stopped playing. All eyes turned to the front of the room, where Mavis, the ball chairman, resplendent in her usual mauve satin gown and matching fan, thanked everyone for their support of the Harvest Ball and introduced Dr. Myers. There was a loud round of applause for the popular physician. He held up his hands to quiet the crowd, which at this point had done a great deal of imbibing and would probably have applauded a spider crawling up a wall.

"Thank you, friends," said the good doctor. "What I say will be brief, but very important. Thanks to all of your wonderful contributions to this year's raffle, we have raised over three thousand dollars for the clinic fund!" This time the applause was sincere and heartfelt. "Wait." He held up his hand again. "I would like to make a surprise announcement. Several weeks ago I was approached by a newcomer to our community, who expressed an interest to me in helping make our new children's wing a reality. He wrote me this check, with the amount left blank, and told me to fill in whatever sum was necessary to make up the difference." He paused. "I would like to thank that very generous person right now, even though he informed me he preferred to remain anonymous. I think by now you have all guessed the man's identity. Mr. Chase Winfield!"

The spotlight combed the crowd and rested on his face. She could tell that he was embarrassed by the attention, and by the thunderous applause that erupted. People kept coming up to him, slapping him on the back or shaking his hand. Some of the older women even kissed him. It was difficult for Diana not to break into a smile. She had to admit that his act of philanthropy had come as quite a surprise to her. Well, maybe it was tax deductible, she thought sarcastically.

Chase started to make his way back to Diana, but didn't get very far. In the first place, Ricky Schuyler kept whisking her away for "just one more dance," and in the second place, he was constantly besieged by well-wishers who wanted to thank him personally for his thoughtfulness.

All too soon, the band was finishing up its last number.

"Would you like me to drive you home?" Ricky asked with a glimmer in his periwinkle eyes. "We could stop off somewhere and maybe I could run out of gas."

Diana laughed good-naturedly. "You'll never change, you smoothie!"

"Well, how about it, Di?" he insisted. "Are you sure I can't persuade you to drive home with me?"

"I'm sorry," interrupted a deep voice. "But she's already promised to let me take her home, young man."

"I did no such thing!" she protested to Chase.

"Darling." He put his arm around her, making his claim on her quite evident to Ricky and anyone else who happened to be standing nearby. "You forgot that Pete asked me to take you home."

Ricky looked quite flustered. "Gee, Mr. Winfield. I didn't know that you and Diana were—I mean . . ." He looked like a schoolboy who had just been caught with his hand in the cookie jar. Poor Ricky. Despite his good looks and easy charm he was simply out of his depth when compared to Chase. The young man melted away tactfully, and Diana was left standing alone with Chase.

"How dare you make up a story like that?" she demanded angrily.

"I didn't hear you object a second time," he countered coolly, steering her toward the exit.

"But Pete—" she began.

"I already told Pete I was taking you back in my car." He led her outside firmly. The night air had become quite chilly, and as they walked toward the parking lot Diana began to shiver beneath her thin gown.

"Are you cold?" he murmured, drawing her close to him.

"N-no," she lied.

"Such a terrible liar!" he declared, removing his tuxedo jacket and placing it around her shoulders.

"Thank you," she replied, unable to conceal the chattering of her teeth.

He unlocked the door to his car. "Do you know why you're so cold, Diana?" He ran a single finger down the center of her gown, pausing directly between her unconfined breasts. "It's because you aren't wearing anything under that delectable little scrap of a dress." He paused. "All night long I've been imagining what's underneath!" Reaching past her, he opened the passenger door and waited for Diana to slide inside. He walked around the car and got comfortably into the driver's seat. He sat there silently for a moment.

It was dark outside in the parking area. For all intents and purposes they were quite alone. Diana looked down at the floor nervously.

"Shy?" he whispered softly.

Diana couldn't answer him. She absently fingered the smooth material of his jacket.

"Come here!" He pulled her suddenly into his lap, and the short dress hiked halfway up her thighs. "Just look at you," he muttered hoarsely, resting a hand several inches above her knee and moving even higher. "You're driving me crazy, do you know that?"

What did he think he was doing to her? The heat from his touch burned its way straight down to the core of her being. There was something both tantalizing and wicked about the way she half-sat, half-lay across his lap, aware of a male passion that Chase was unable to conceal in his present position.

"Feel what you do to me, little mermaid?" he rasped.

"I thought you were going to drive me home," she reproved breathlessly.

"Just one more minute!" he groaned. "Let me just hold you now!" He tipped her head back and took her lower lip between his teeth gently. Keeping one hand firmly on her thigh, he let his free hand travel down the side of her neck. "I could eat you," he whispered. "You taste so incredibly delicious." He plunged his lips against the base of her throat, blazing a liquid fire back up toward her throbbing mouth.

"Don't!" she protested, suddenly remembering the blonde in the boat. She mustn't let him do this, she mused, wreak havoc on her senses and then leave her wanting more.

"You shouldn't fight me, love!" he said thickly, pulling her to him in a searing kiss, drinking in every last drop of sweetness in her mouth. "Like honey!" Chase declared between kisses. "Don't you dare let any other bee around my flower, do you hear?" A hand came around to touch her bare back. "Was he the one you went out with two nights ago?"

She struggled against him. "Whom are you talking about?"

Chase's eyes narrowed. "That young pup . . . the one who's built like a linebacker. The one who was all over you on the dance floor tonight!"

She shrugged. "Oh, do you mean Ricky Schuyler? As it so happens, he *is* a linebacker."

"I'm not surprised," came the caustic reply. "They have notoriously thick skulls!" Chase forced her chin upward. "If I ever see you with him again, I'll beat him to a pulp." He paused. "On the other hand, I'll have a different kind of punishment for you. The first thing I'll do is—"

He began to whisper a series of things so intimate and sensual that Diana gasped in shock. "Don't say such things!" she exclaimed, flushing bright crimson and once again attempting to squirm free from his grasp. His behavior tonight completely baffled her. Last evening he had announced his intention of just remaining friends. Then he had made passionate love to her, tearing himself away when things threatened to get out of hand. Yet now he was feasting his hungry mouth on her as if she were a chocolate cake he was devouring layer by layer.

"God, I want you!" he groaned. "Let's go home right now!" He set her away from him reluctantly and turned on the ignition. He thrust the car into gear and peeled out of the parking lot.

In less than ten minutes he pulled the Mercedes into her driveway. Without a word he walked around to the passenger side and drew her out of the seat. His hands cupped the sides of her face, and he gazed at her with raw hunger. "You're mine," he uttered thickly. "You're mine and I intend to have you!"

She couldn't permit this to continue. In another minute he'd be carrying her upstairs to bed and she would be lost. No matter how much her heart and her body cried out for Chase at this very minute, she could not allow herself to be swept along on this reckless tide. Afterward, how could she bear to be left with the wreckage of her love? She would never be able to share him with all his other women. Better to cut it off now, before the destruction was final.

His arms drew her up against him, and firm hands traveled down her bare back to rest possessively upon her buttocks. He shook his head. "How could I have been such a fool as to push you away from me? I ache all over for you." The naked passion in his voice rocked Diana like an earthquake, but then she remembered that there were many other women he ached for. It was like a bucket of cold water washing down over her, dampening Diana's own desire.

"Get away from me!" she cried out. "Leave me alone, I don't want you!" She tore herself away from him. "I'm not like that—that woman you've been seeing."

He froze dead in his tracks. "What are you talking about?"

Diana averted her eyes so that he wouldn't be able to read the pain in them. "I was down by the water. I saw you and your girlfriend in that boat of yours."

He didn't say anything, but to Diana his silence spoke louder than a thousand words.

"Yes," she blurted out with a quiver. "Your silence is deafening."

Slowly, he released her and stepped back away. "I don't suppose an explanation would matter very much at this point."

"I don't suppose it would," she agreed bitterly.

He sighed and thrust his hands into his pockets. "Because you probably wouldn't believe anything I told you right now, would you, Diana?"

She couldn't even look at him. "Just go away!" Her voice was hollow.

"Then there's nothing more to be said," he replied dully. "I'd better just leave."

Diana didn't answer him. Even as he started down

the steps, and something within her screamed for him to come back, she forced herself to remain silent. She waited till he reached his car and swung the door open. It was then she realized he was probably never coming back.

Please, Chase Winfield, she begged in a voice only she could hear. *Please, don't ever come back! Let me get over you as best I can!*

Diana could hear the car roaring out of the driveway, and something wet touched her upper lip. It wasn't until that very moment she realized she was crying.

Chapter Ten

Diana spent the next morning at the recreation hall, helping clean up the debris from the previous night's revels. It wasn't a chore she particularly relished, but it was expected that all committee members help take down the decorations and restore the hall to its former neatness. Naturally, the conversation leaned heavily on the subject of Chase Winfield and his unprecedented donation to the clinic. Also, to her chagrin, a great many comments were made concerning Diana, her dress, and Chase Winfield's obvious interest in both. Two hours of this was just about all she could take, and after helping load two dozen plastic trash bags into the dumpster, Diana went back outside to her car. It had started to rain just an hour before, but now the droplets were coming down more heavily. This didn't particularly bother Diana. She liked the rain. There was something so enveloping, so very soothing about it.

About a mile before the turnoff for her driveway, the car drifted to a stop. One look at the gas gauge told her what the problem was. Never in her entire five years behind the wheel had she ever been careless enough to drive on an empty tank. But considering the inner turmoil that had afflicted her in the past few weeks, she was hardly surprised that this was the result. Fortunately, the car now rested on a grassy if wet patch of shoulder. At least it wouldn't be blocking the path of any other vehicles.

She emerged into the rain, and sighed at the prospect of more than a mile hike home. Lowering her head against the downpour, she began to walk briskly along the side of the road. The rain was growing even more heavy, soaking her to the skin, the water running in rivulets down her face. She shivered and increased her pace. The problem now was that the shower had become so strong, she could barely see a foot in front of her. There was no way she saw the oncoming car, but she heard it swerve and screech to a stop. A door slammed.

Two hard hands gripped her shoulders. "Are you crazy?" Chase roared at her above the noise of the storm. "You nearly got yourself killed just now! If I hadn't seen you in time—"

"What were you doing in the middle of the road?" she shouted back at him.

"I skidded to avoid hitting you!" he thundered back, his face a mask of black fury.

She had never seen him so enraged. "What was I supposed to do? My car broke down back there. I had to walk. Can I help it if I happened to get stuck in a blinding rain?"

He didn't answer her; he was too busy taking in her bedraggled appearance. "Why, you're soaked to the skin!" Without waiting for a reply he scooped her up in his arms and threw her into the backseat of the Mercedes. "There's a blanket in there," he informed her tersely. "Wrap yourself in it before you catch pneumonia."

She was too cold, too wet, just too altogether miserable not to obey him.

"We're closer to my place than to yours," he continued in an emotionless voice, steering the car in the opposite direction and pulling into his own long driveway. He drove the car practically up the front steps. Then, without so much as another word, he lifted her gently up in his arms and carried her up to the front door. He set her down on her feet while he unlocked the entrance. A moment later he was carrying her inside the main hall.

The house looked completely different from the way it had three weeks ago. The dust covers were off the furniture and all the packing crates had vanished. With numerous valuable Persian rugs and plants everywhere she looked, Grey Lodge now resembled a home. Chase silently climbed the long staircase with Diana still held high in his arms. After passing through one door, and then another, she found herself first in a large bedroom, and then the spacious bathroom.

"I'm going to get you out of those wet clothes," he muttered, "and then I'm putting you into a hot tub." Chase began to pull the soaking T-shirt over Diana's head.

"No!" she protested. "I can do this myself!"

He stopped what he was doing. "Very well. But hurry up before you catch a chill." Chase leaned over the sunken tub with gold-handled spigots and turned on the faucets full force. His expression was hooded and unreadable. "I'll be right outside. Call me when you've finished." He turned and walked out of the bathroom, shutting the door behind him.

Diana sank into the warm water and shut her eyes as it lapped around her soothingly. For a minute she forgot where she was and whose bathtub she was soaking in. But when she remembered, it suddenly didn't matter. This was the place she wanted to be. Despite the numerous pitfalls in a relationship with Chase Winfield, she realized that she would rather be miserable with him than miserable without him. It was as simple as that. Her decision was made at that exact moment. She rose from the tub slowly and wrapped herself in one of the huge fleecy white towels that hung from a brass ring by the door. After rubbing her dark hair dry with a towel, she found a tortoise-shell comb on the counter by the sink and ran it through her tresses until they hung down straight and shiny, without a single tangle.

Taking a deep breath, she opened the door slowly and entered the bedroom. Chase looked up from the magazine he sat reading in a rocking chair by the window.

"Are you warm now, Diana?" he asked quietly. Odd, but she only now noticed the dark circles under his eyes.

She took a step toward him. "No, I'm still cold."

He rose quickly to his feet. "Let me get you a robe!" he exclaimed.

"I don't want a robe," she said softly. "The only thing that can keep me warm right now is you, Chase."

"What?" he whispered. "What did you just say to me?"

She tore her eyes away from him, unable to let him read the vulnerability in them. "Warm me, Chase."

His voice was oddly distant. "After everything I've done you still want me?"

"I can't help it," she confessed unashamedly. "I love you too much."

"You what?" he boomed, flying across the room in two short strides. "Say that again!" He gripped her bare shoulders violently.

"I love you, Chase," Diana whispered, almost relieved that her secret was out in the open at last.

"Oh, Diana" he groaned. "My sweet little

mermaid . . ." Chase's eyes glittered silver-gray as he shook his head over and over again. "I don't believe it. You actually love me?" He cupped her face in his hands with exquisite tenderness. "It's been that way for me since that night on the beach, when a creature from a wonderful fairy tale walked back into my life." He reached down and kissed her forehead and her eyelids. "Are you sure?" He kissed her cheeks and then her earlobes. "You really love me?" He kissed apart her lips and probed the moistness inside with a ravenous tongue.

"Chase!" she exclaimed breathlessly.

"I'm going to kiss you till you scream for mercy, little mermaid!" he murmured huskily. "After all the tortures you've put me through!"

"What about the tortures you put *me* through, you beast?" she cried out.

He tightened his arms around her. "I couldn't make love to you, darling, even though I ached. I couldn't take what you so sweetly offered me. You were a virgin, and it would have been criminal to take what I wanted so badly until you were sure about your feelings for me." He brushed the hair out of her eyes. "I knew you wanted me, Diana. I knew about the incredible physical attraction between us. But I had to give you time to fully understand what you were feeling. It meant too much to me."

"You truly care for me, Chase?" She shook her head incredulously. "I never thought—"

"Hush, darling." He placed a gentle hand over her lips and led her to the bed. "I want you to sit down while I tell you something—several things, in fact. There are a few misunderstandings that must be cleared up now." He drew her into his lap and leaned back against the oak headboard. "Do you know why I left you so abruptly last night?"

She looked away uncomfortably. "Do we have to talk about that?" The very thought of the other woman in Chase's life was ruining this very wonderful moment.

"I didn't stay to explain about Sonya—that's the woman whom you saw me with yesterday. I couldn't stay. I knew you were too hurt and angry to believe anything I might have told you. But the truth is, Sonya is no longer part of my life. She hasn't been for over a year. The fact of the matter is, Sonya invited herself up to the lake, and not the other way around. I took her out in the boat and tried to let her down as gently as possible." He stroked Diana's hair. "I put her on the helicopter back to the airport an hour later." He paused. "I didn't want her around. I didn't want anything or anyone intruding on what I had with you. Please believe me, love."

She gazed up at him with trusting eyes. "I believe you," she whispered.

Chase continued to stroke her. "The reason why I've been buying up all the property on the lake, the one I said was too personal to discuss. Now I can tell you." He smiled slowly. "That night five years ago, when you pulled me from the water, I was enchanted. No matter what I did or where I went over the years I kept returning in my mind to that magical night." He sighed. "You see, the lake represented a lost dream. I knew there could be no such thing as a mermaid, yet the associations from the experience were still with me. That's why I bought Grey Lodge. I knew it was the one place in the world that would always be magic to me somehow. I couldn't bear the thought of that magic being destroyed by developers one day, so I set out to preserve the lake by buying it up for myself."

Diana's eyes widened. "You bought Grey Lodge because of—"

"Because of you, my little mermaid. That wonderful night on the beach when I realized you truly existed, I couldn't believe my good fortune. I was never going to let you go after that." He buried his face against her neck. "It's been hell these past two weeks. I know I've botched it rather badly, but I didn't know what to do from one moment to the next. I've never been in love before."

When she looked back on it later on, Diana realized that this was the happiest moment of her life. She would always cherish the memory of Chase holding her in his arms on the huge bed while the rain poured down furiously outside.

"Will you be moving back to San Francisco?" she asked many kisses later.

"In the first place, my little mermaid, *I* am not doing anything anymore. It is *we.* And after we're married, we can live wherever you want. I don't care."

"After we're *what?*"

His eyes narrowed into silver slits. "You slippery little sea creature!" he declared with darkening passion. "You honestly don't think I'm going to let you get away after it's taken me so long to catch you!" He slowly slid the towel open. "It's like unwrapping a birthday present," he whispered hotly. "You're so beautiful—shiny and new!"

"Are you going to play with me now?" she teased gently.

His breath quickened. "Oh, Diana. I love you." Chase started at her hair and began kissing his way down her naked body. When he reached her breasts she moaned in pleasure, and he teased each peak to hardness and did not stop until she arched against him, begging for a new kind of satisfaction. He continued to blaze a trail of desire down across her smooth, flat stomach, and then he was touching her in secret places she had never been touched before, arousing her to heights of excitement Diana had never even imagined.

"What I said that night," he groaned, "about taking my time with you—"

She wrapped her arms around his neck and pulled him down against her silky bare skin. The only barrier between them were his blue jeans. "Time is something we have plenty of, darling!"

Suddenly, he tore himself away from her and rose from the bed. "Don't go anywhere!" he ordered thickly. "Don't even move!"

"Where are you—" She sat up quickly.

But Chase was back in a flash with a small package

that he picked up from the nightstand. "I have two presents I've been waiting to give you." He sat back down on the bed, handing her the box that was wrapped in gold paper.

"You say you've been *waiting* to give me this?" she asked, puzzled.

"Open it," he whispered softly. "I was going to give it to you last night, after the dance, but then it was too late."

She unwrapped the package to find a velvet jeweler's box. The lid snapped open. "Oh, Chase!" she exclaimed, lifting out two exquisite antique silver combs with elaborate scrollwork along the crowns.

"I bought them three weeks ago, when I had to fly back to San Francisco. I thought of you the moment I saw them."

"They're beautiful," she said with a quiver. "Will you put them on for me?"

He took the mermaid combs and slid one carefully onto a strand of hair on each side of her head. "Let that be the only thing you wear," he uttered hoarsely as he began to touch her again.

She smiled. "You said you had *two* presents."

"That's quite true," he murmured, moving his long, hard body against hers. "I was just about to give you the other one!"

READERS' COMMENTS ON SILHOUETTE ROMANCES:

"The best time of my day is when I put my children to bed at naptime and sit down to read a Silhouette Romance. Keep up the good work."

P.M.*, Allegan, MI

"I am very fond of the quality of your Silhouette Romances. They are so real. I have tried to read some of the other romances, but I always come back to Silhouette."

C.S., Mechanicsburg, PA

"I feel that Silhouette Books offer a wider choice and/or variety than any of the other romance books available."

R.R., Aberdeen, WA

"I have enjoyed reading Silhouette Romances for many years now. They are light and refreshing. You can always put yourself in the main characters' place, feeling alive and beautiful."

J.M.K., San Antonio, TX

"My boyfriend always teases me about Silhouette Books. He asks me, how's my love life and naturally I say terrific, but I tell him that there is always room for a little more romance from Silhouette."

F.N., Ontario, Canada

*names available on request

READERS' COMMENTS ON SILHOUETTE DESIRES

"Thank you for Silhouette Desires. They are the best thing that has happened to the bookshelves in a long time."

—V.W.*, Knoxville, TN

"Silhouette Desires—wonderful, fantastic—the best romance around."

—H.T.*, Margate, N.J.

"As a writer as well as a reader of romantic fiction, I found DESIREs most refreshingly realistic—and definitely as magical as the love captured on their pages."

—C.M.*, Silver Lake, N.Y.

"I just wanted to let you know how very much I enjoy your Silhouette Desire books. I read other romances, and I must say your books rate up at the top of the list."

—C.N.*, Anaheim, CA

"Desires are number one. I especially enjoy the endings because they just don't leave you with a kiss or embrace; they finish the story. Thank you for giving me such reading pleasure."

—M.S.*, Sandford, FL

*names available on request

RCD

READERS' COMMENTS ON SILHOUETTE SPECIAL EDITIONS:

"I just finished reading the first six Silhouette Special Edition Books and I had to take the opportunity to write you and tell you how much I enjoyed them. I enjoyed all the authors in this series. Best wishes on your Silhouette Special Editions line and many thanks."

—B.H.*, Jackson, OH

"The Special Editions are really special and I enjoyed them very much! I am looking forward to next month's books."

—R.M.W.*, Melbourne, FL

"I've just finished reading four of your first six Special Editions and I enjoyed them very much. I like the more sensual detail and longer stories. I will look forward each month to your new Special Editions."

—L.S.*, Visalia, CA

"Silhouette Special Editions are — 1.) Superb! 2.) Great! 3.) Delicious! 4.) Fantastic! . . . Did I leave anything out? These are books that an adult woman can read . . . I love them!"

—H.C.*, Monterey Park, CA

*names available on request